The
Riverdale
Diaries

Hello, Betty!

BuzzPop

For my dad—see, it *was* worth it
to buy me all those comics
—SK

To my nieces and nephews
—JB

An imprint of Little Bee Books
251 Park Avenue South, New York, NY 10010
Copyright © 2020 by Archie Comic Publications, Inc.
All rights reserved, including the right of reproduction
in whole or in part in any form. BuzzPop and associated
colophon are trademarks of Little Bee Books.
Lettering by Hannah McGill

Library of Congress Cataloging-in-Publication Data
is available upon request.
Manufactured in China RRD 0520
First Edition
ISBN 978-1-4998-1055-4 (hc)
2 4 6 8 10 9 7 5 3 1
ISBN 978-1-4998-1054-7 (pb)
2 4 6 8 10 9 7 5 3 1

buzzpopbooks.com

For more information about special discounts on bulk purchases,
please contact Little Bee Books at sales@littlebeebooks.com.

THE CAST

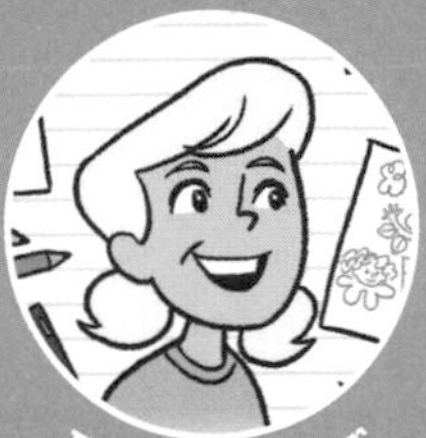
Betty Cooper
the writer

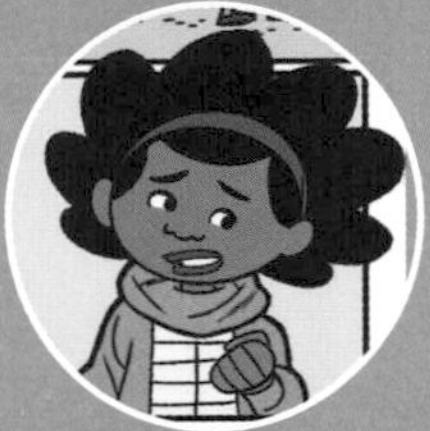
Val Smith
the rock star

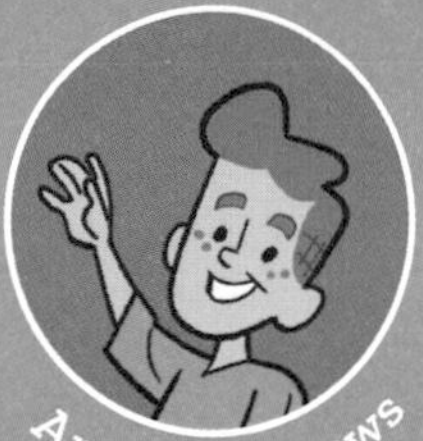
Archie Andrews
the clumsy kid

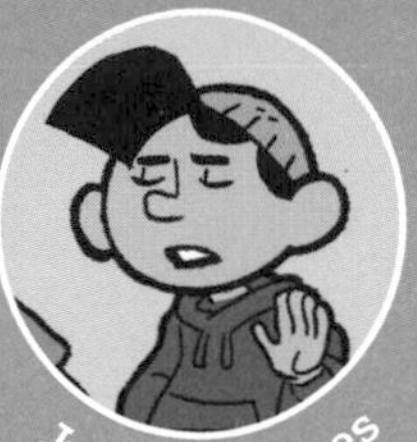
Jughead Jones
the mysterious kid

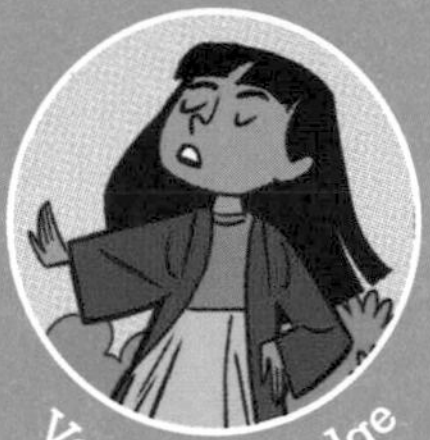
Veronica Lodge
the prima donna

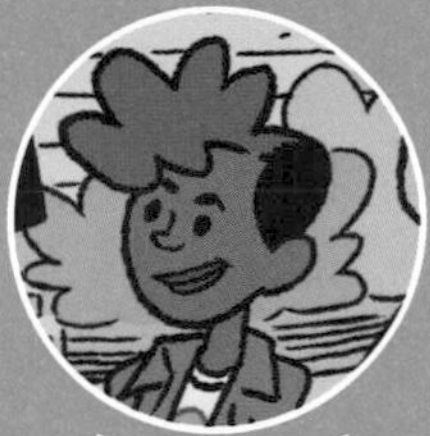
Toni Topaz
the coolest kid in town

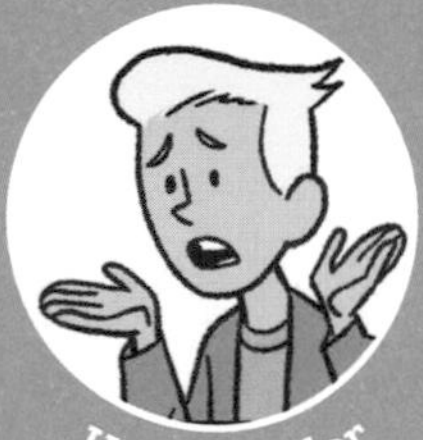
Kevin Keller
the nicest kid in town

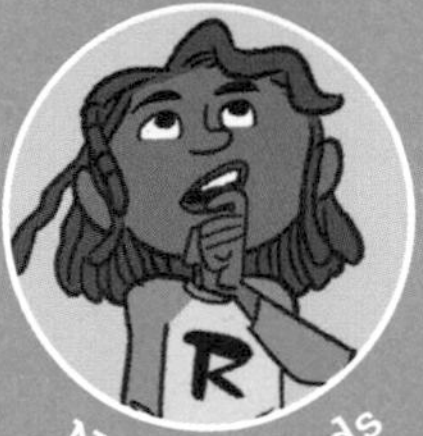
R
Nancy Woods
the jock

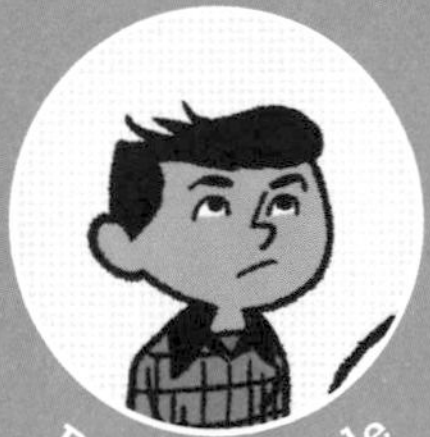
Reggie Mantle
the grumpy kid

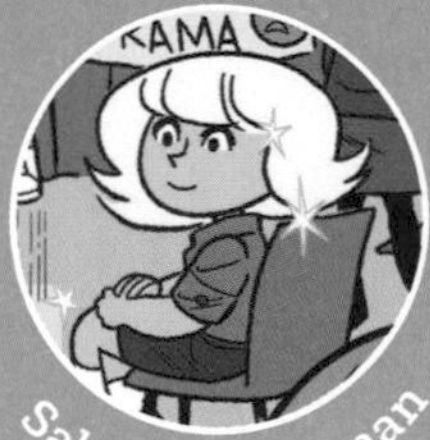
Sabrina Spellman
the magical kid

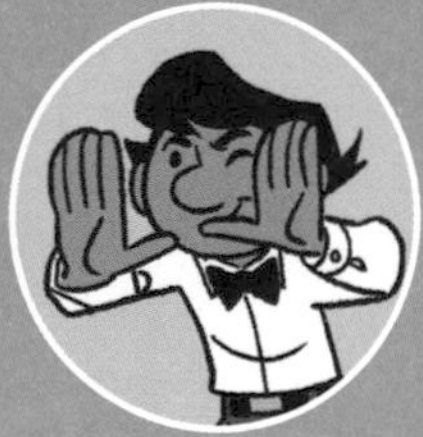
Raj Patel
the visionary

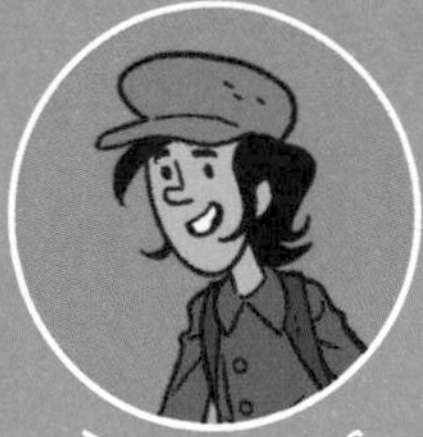
Ethel Muggs
the henchgirl

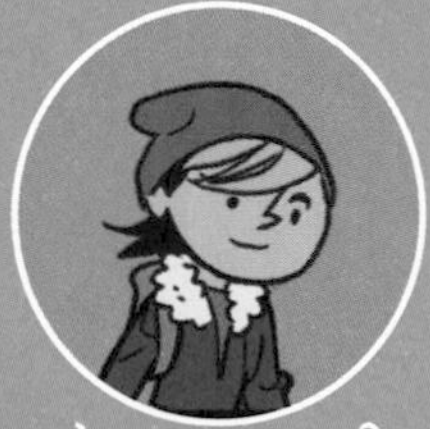
Midge Klump
the other henchgirl

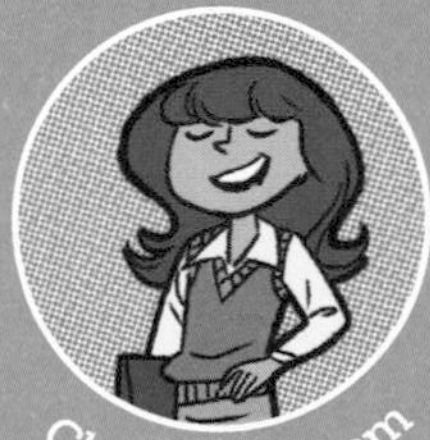
Cheryl Blossom
the older kid

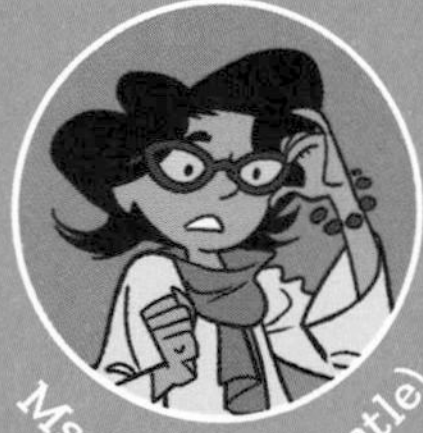
Ms. Vicky (Mantle)
the adult

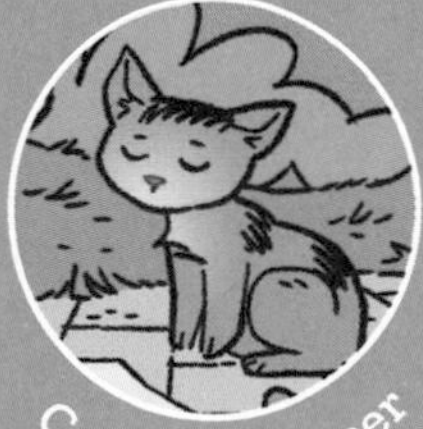
Caramel Cooper
the cat

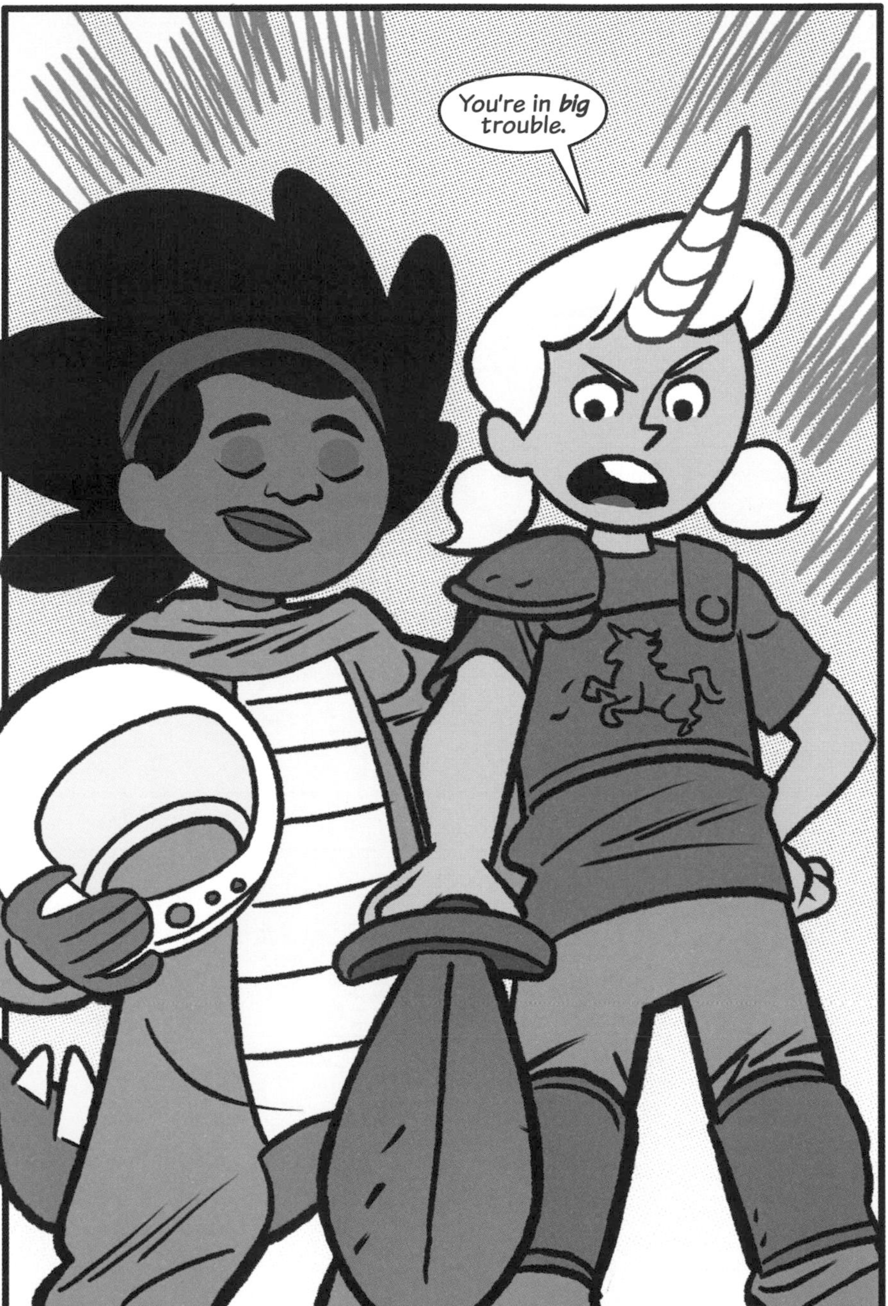
You're in *big* trouble.

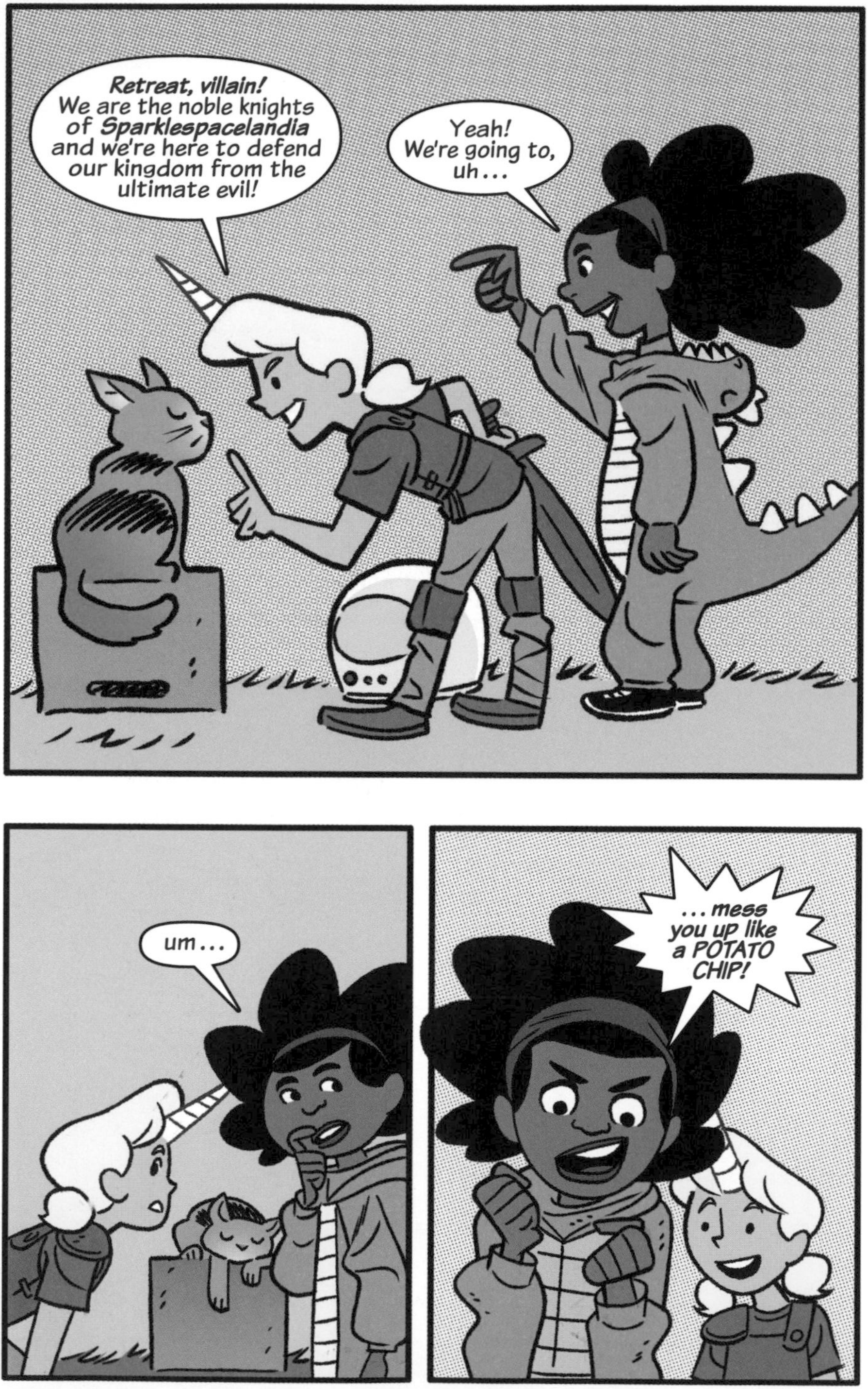
Retreat, villain! We are the noble knights of Sparklespacelandia and we're here to defend our kingdom from the ultimate evil!
Yeah! We're going to, uh...
um...
...mess you up like a POTATO CHIP!

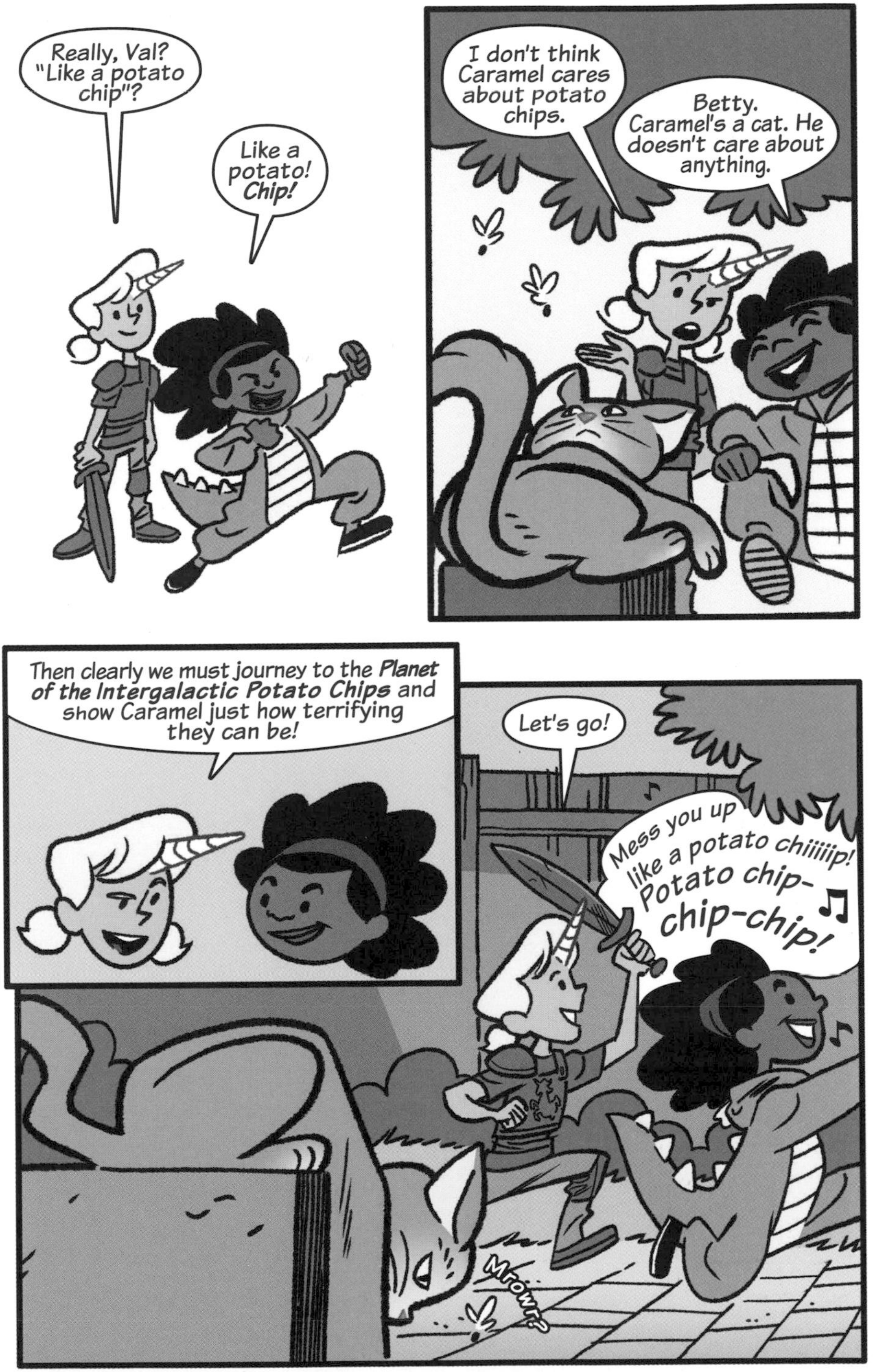
Really, Val? "Like a potato chip"?
Like a potato! *Chip!*
I don't think Caramel cares about potato chips.
Betty. Caramel's a cat. He doesn't care about anything.
Then clearly we must journey to the *Planet of the Intergalactic Potato Chips* and show Caramel just how terrifying they can be!
Let's go!
Mess you up like a potato chiiiiip! Potato chip-chip-chip!
Mrowr?

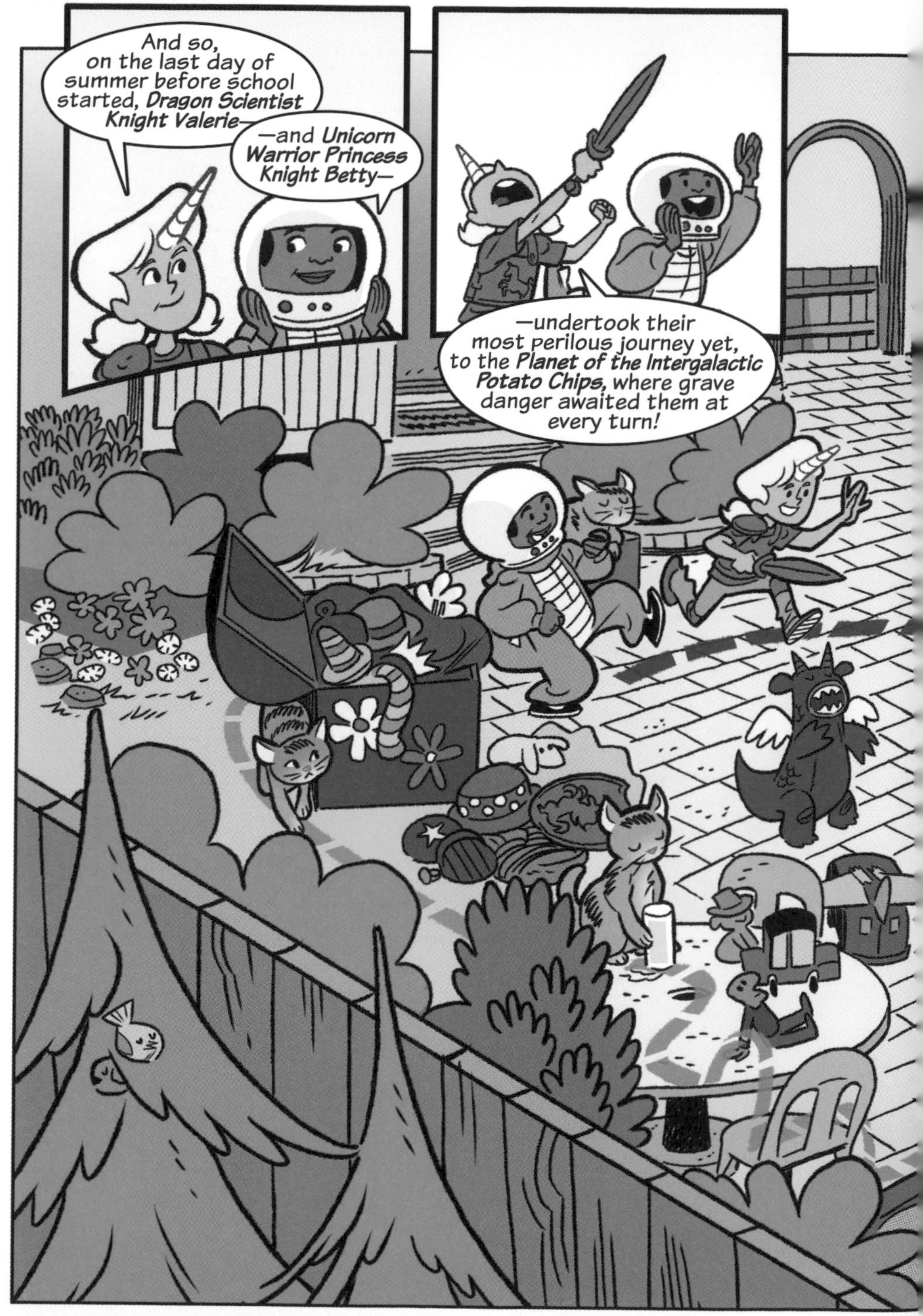
And so, on the last day of summer before school started, *Dragon Scientist Knight Valerie*—
—and *Unicorn Warrior Princess Knight Betty*—
—undertook their most perilous journey yet, to the *Planet of the Intergalactic Potato Chips,* where grave danger awaited them at every turn!

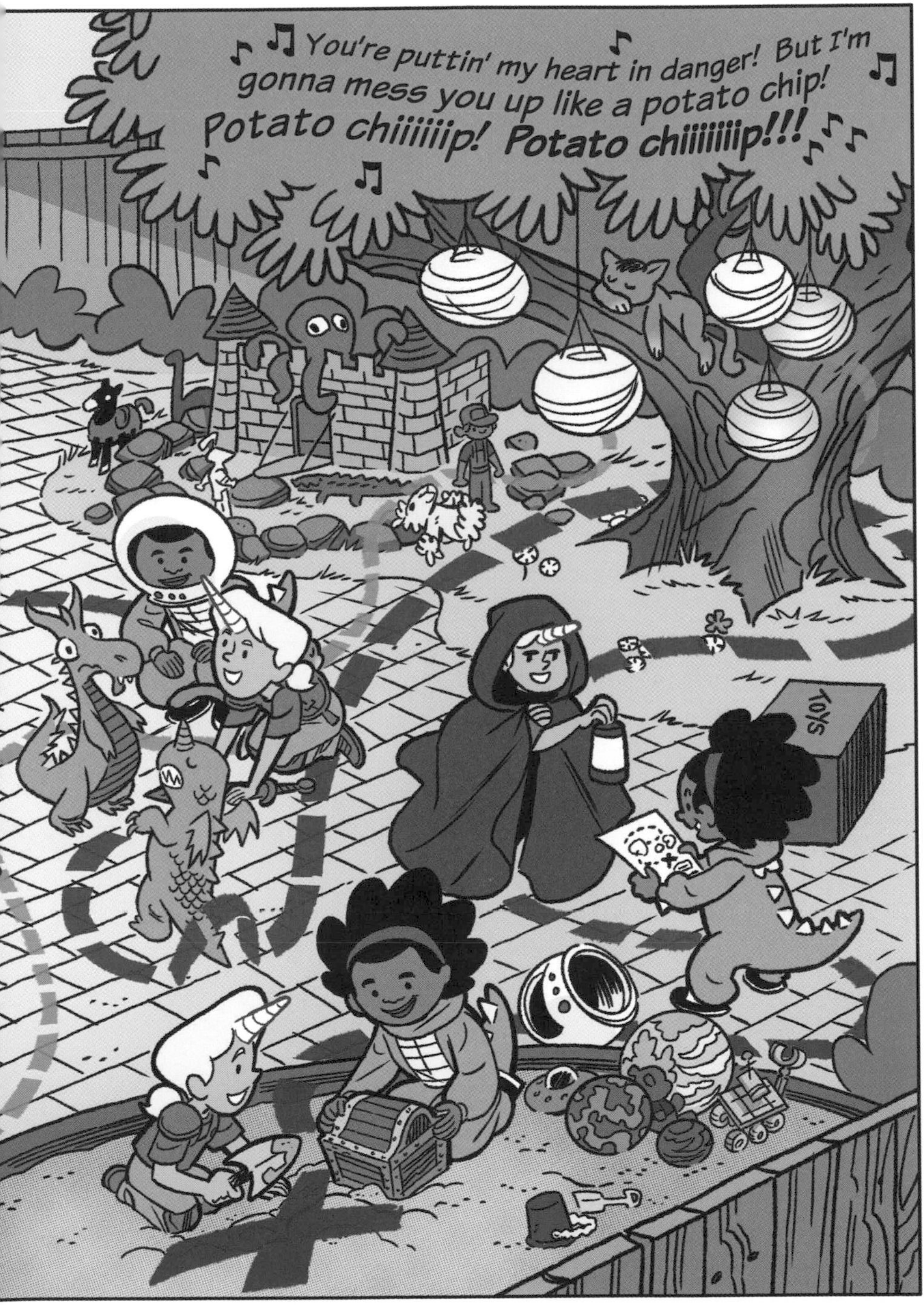
♪ ♫ You're puttin' my heart in danger! But I'm gonna mess you up like a potato chip!
Potato chiiiiiip! Potato chiiiiiip!!!
TOYS

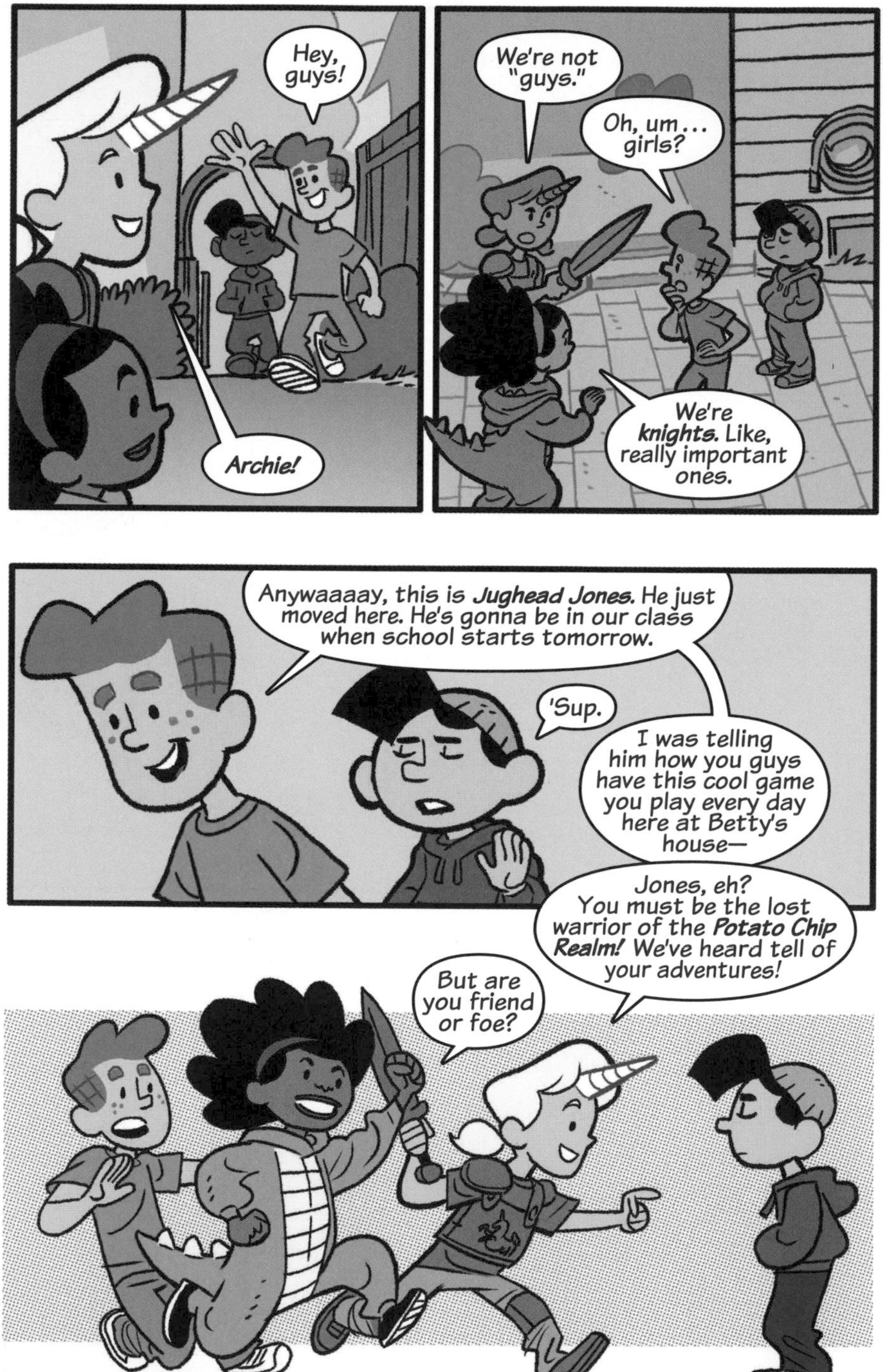

Hey, guys!
Archie!
We're not "guys."
Oh, um... girls?
We're ***knights.*** Like, really important ones.
Anywaaaay, this is ***Jughead Jones.*** He just moved here. He's gonna be in our class when school starts tomorrow.
'Sup.
I was telling him how you guys have this cool game you play every day here at Betty's house—
Jones, eh? You must be the lost warrior of the ***Potato Chip Realm!*** We've heard tell of your adventures!
But are you friend or foe?

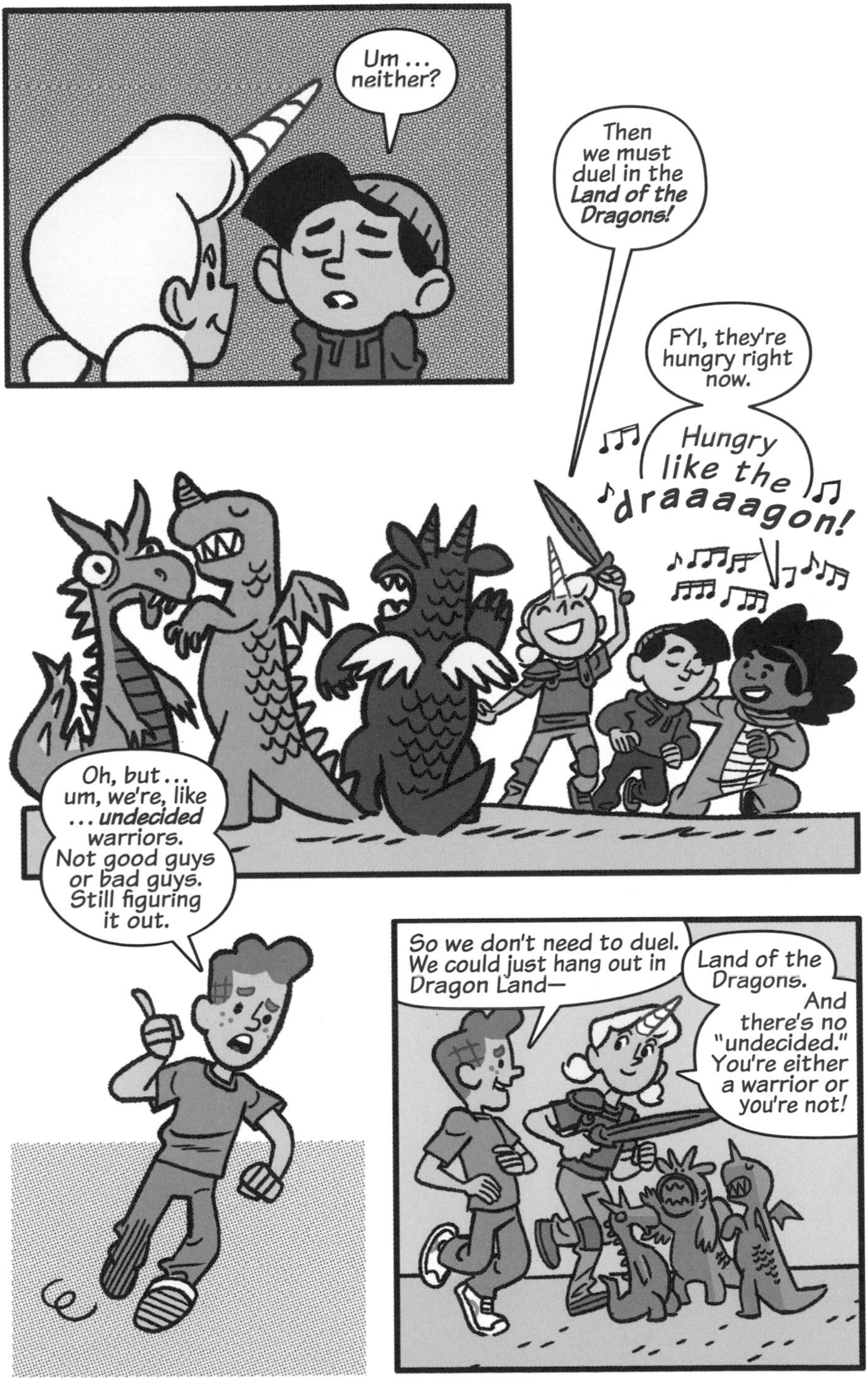
Um ... neither?
Then we must duel in the Land of the Dragons!
FYI, they're hungry right now.
Hungry like the draaaaagon!
Oh, but ... um, we're, like ... undecided warriors. Not good guys or bad guys. Still figuring it out.
So we don't need to duel. We could just hang out in Dragon Land—
Land of the Dragons.
And there's no "undecided." You're either a warrior or you're not!

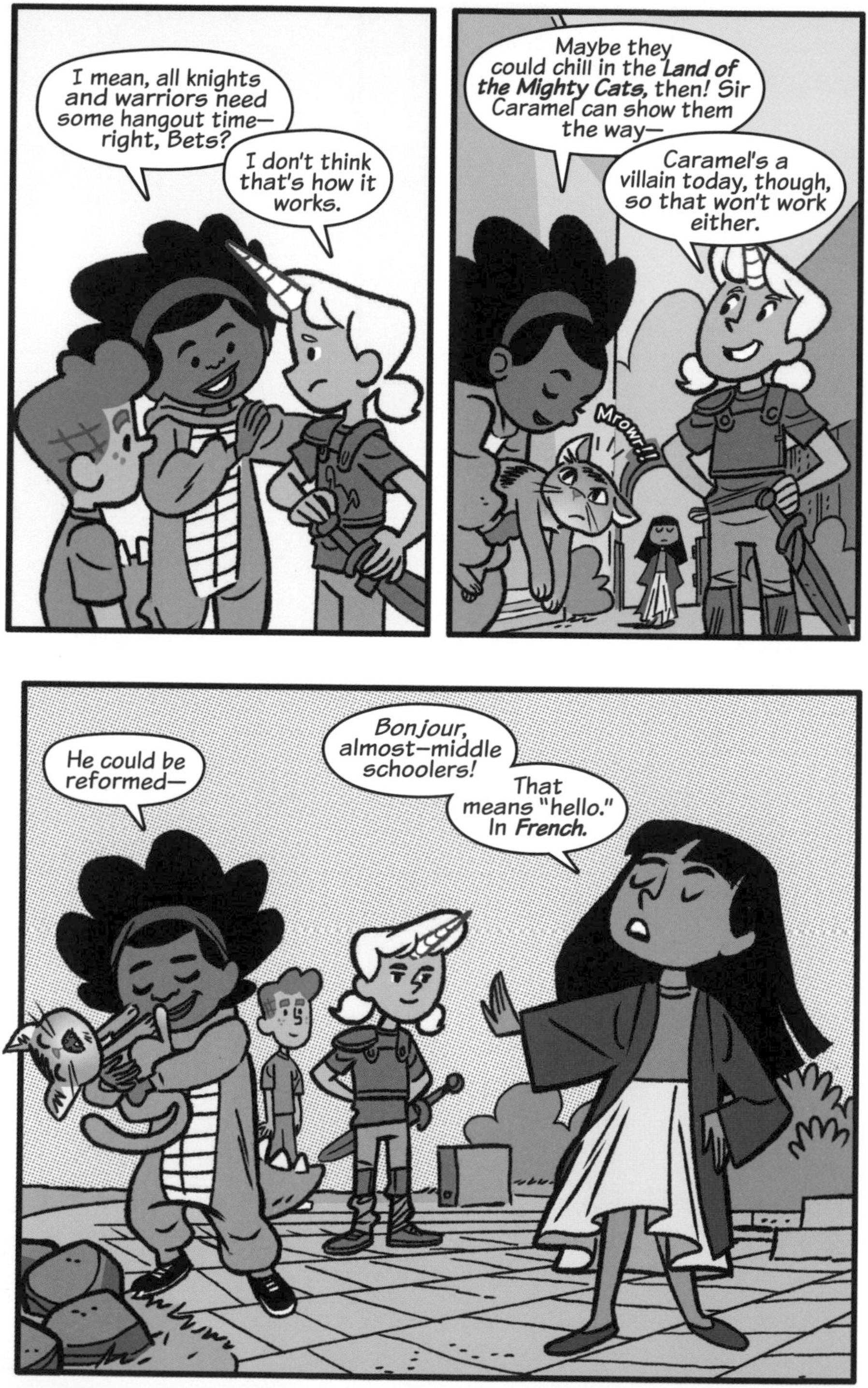
I mean, all knights and warriors need some hangout time—right, Bets?
I don't think that's how it works.
Maybe they could chill in the **Land of the Mighty Cats,** then! Sir Caramel can show them the way—
Caramel's a villain today, though, so that won't work either.
Mrowr!!
He could be reformed—
Bonjour, almost-middle schoolers!
That means "hello." In ***French.***

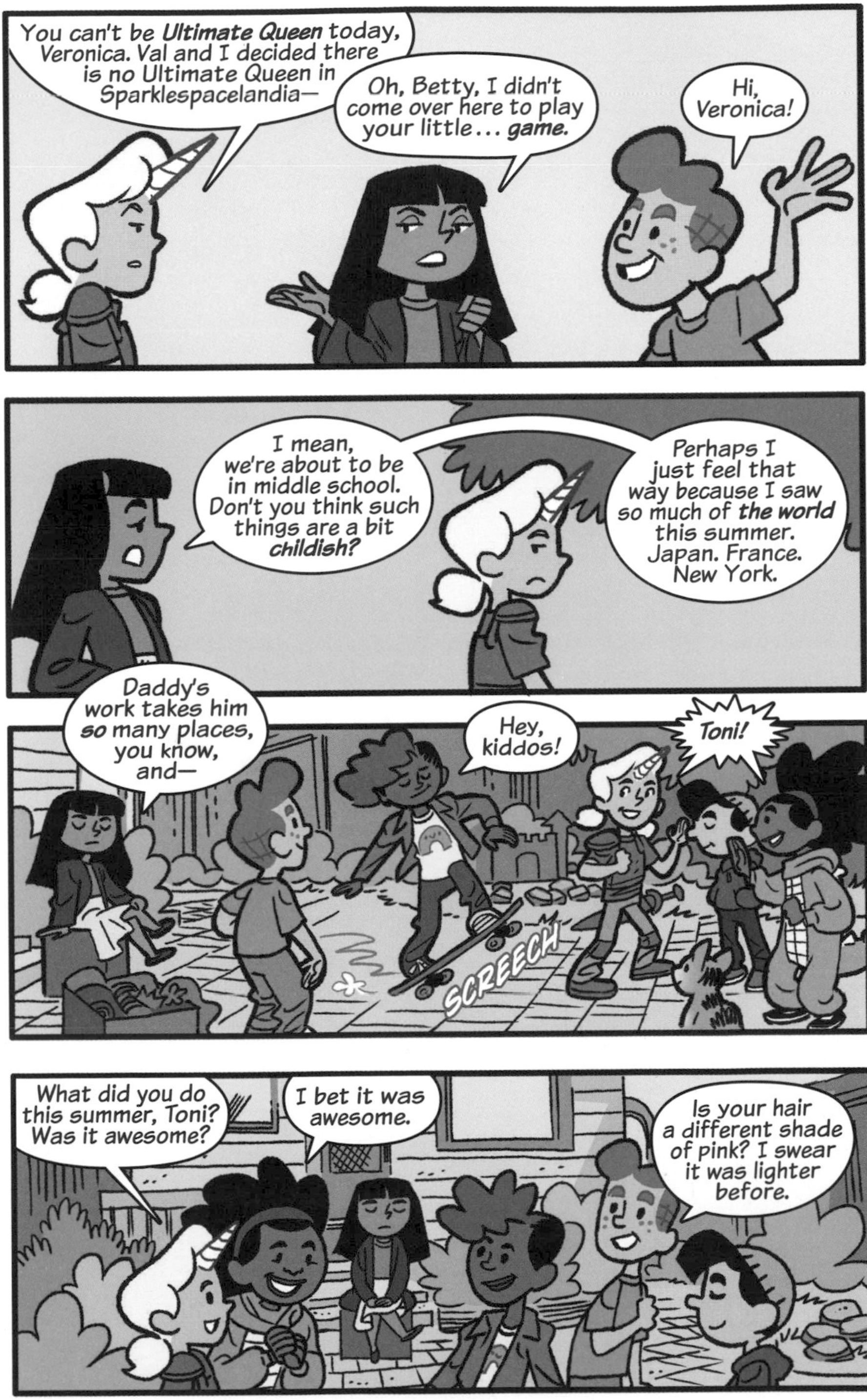
You can't be **Ultimate Queen** today, Veronica. Val and I decided there is no Ultimate Queen in Sparklespacelandia—
Oh, Betty, I didn't come over here to play your little... **game.**
Hi, Veronica!
I mean, we're about to be in middle school. Don't you think such things are a bit **childish?**
Perhaps I just feel that way because I saw so much of **the world** this summer. Japan. France. New York.
Daddy's work takes him **so** many places, you know, and—
Hey, kiddos!
Toni!
SCREECH
What did you do this summer, Toni? Was it awesome?
I bet it was awesome.
Is your hair a different shade of pink? I swear it was lighter before.

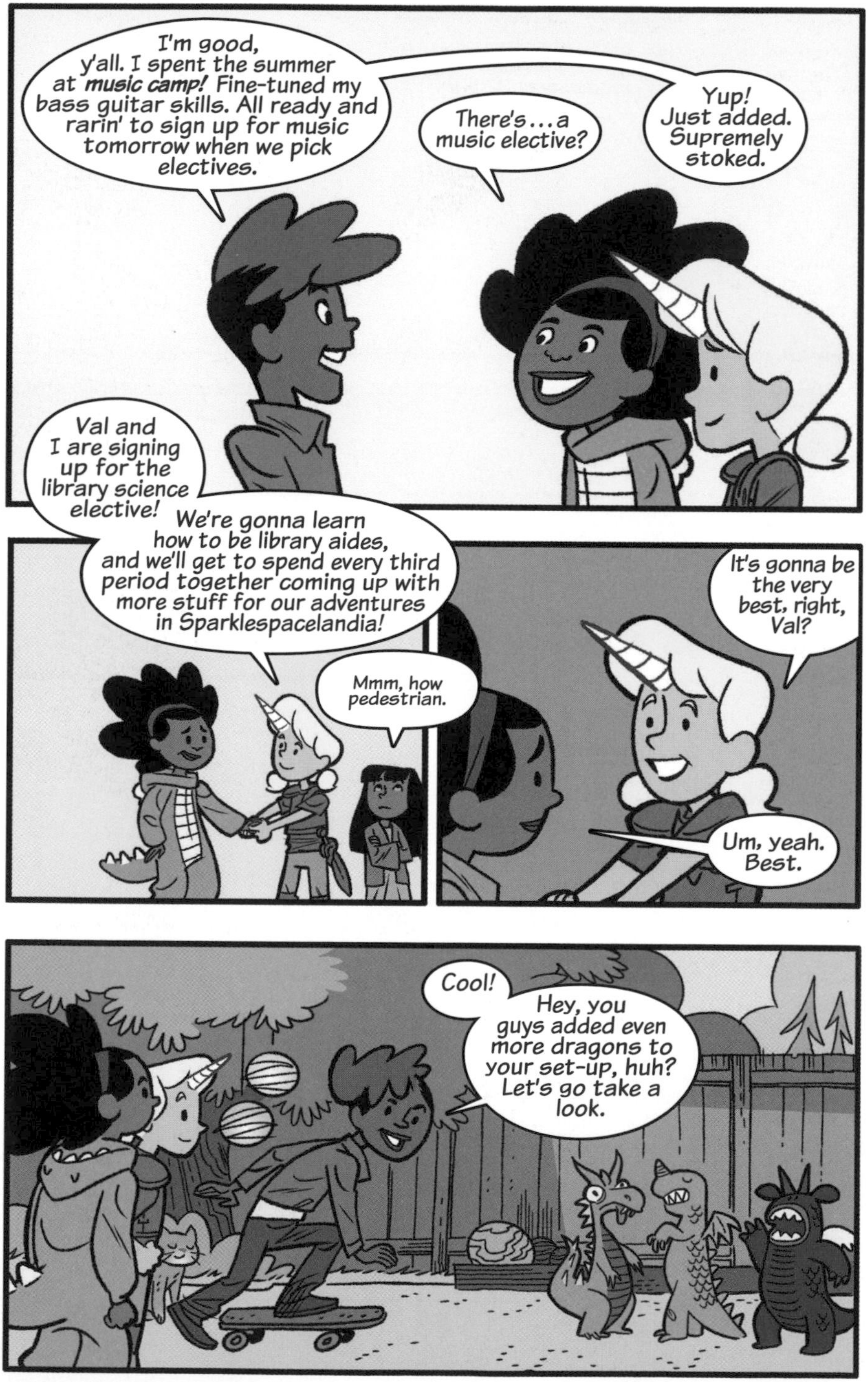

I'm good, y'all. I spent the summer at *music camp!* Fine-tuned my bass guitar skills. All ready and rarin' to sign up for music tomorrow when we pick electives.
There's . . . a music elective?
Yup! Just added. Supremely stoked.
Val and I are signing up for the library science elective!
We're gonna learn how to be library aides, and we'll get to spend every third period together coming up with more stuff for our adventures in Sparklespacelandia!
Mmm, how pedestrian.
It's gonna be the very best, right, Val?
Um, yeah. Best.
Cool!
Hey, you guys added even more dragons to your set-up, huh? Let's go take a look.

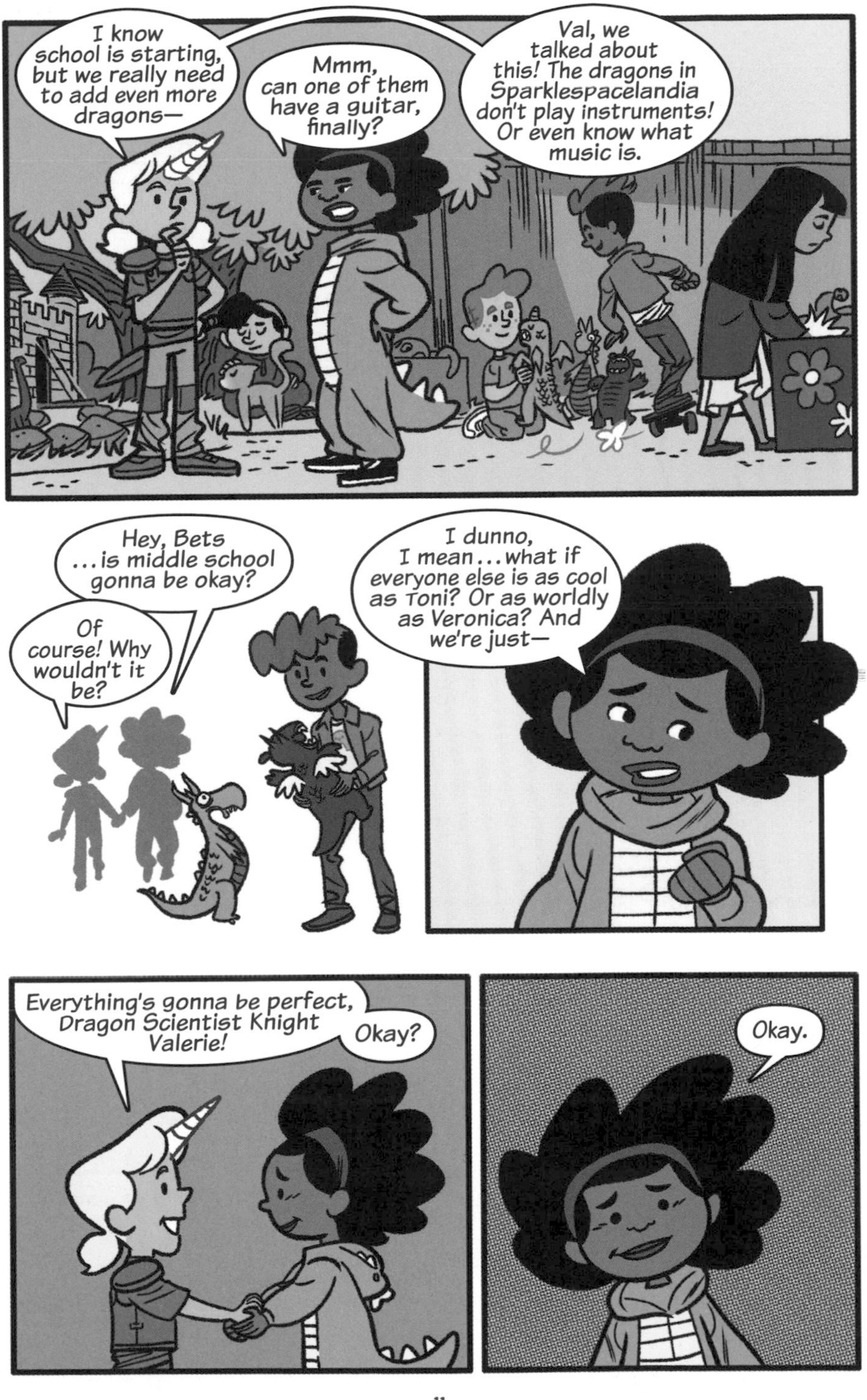
I know school is starting, but we really need to add even more dragons—
Mmm, can one of them have a guitar, finally?
Val, we talked about this! The dragons in Sparklespacelandia don't play instruments! Or even know what music is.
Hey, Bets ...is middle school gonna be okay?
Of course! Why wouldn't it be?
I dunno, I mean...what if everyone else is as cool as Toni? Or as worldly as Veronica? And we're just—
Everything's gonna be perfect, Dragon Scientist Knight Valerie!
Okay?
Okay.

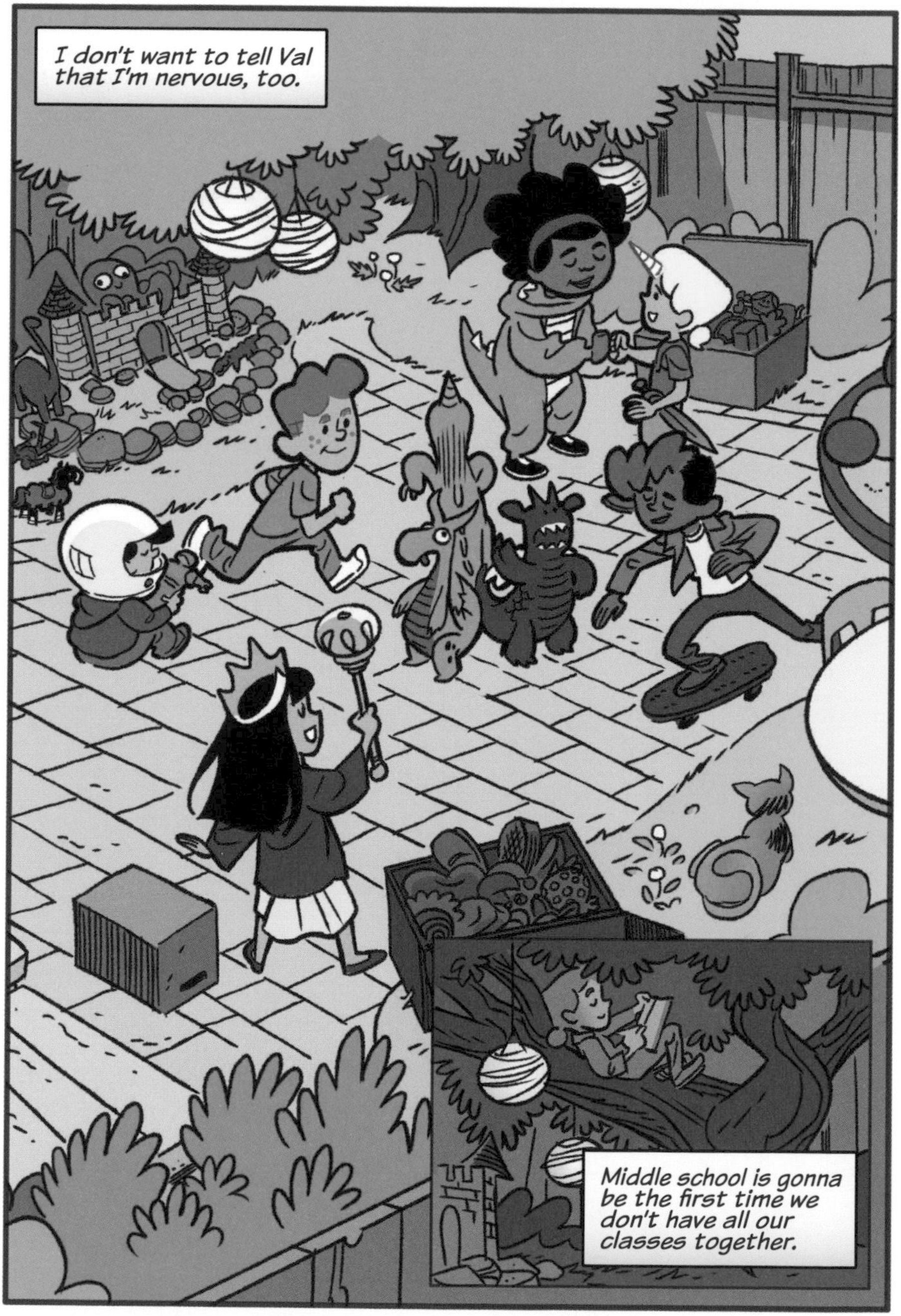
I don't want to tell Val that I'm nervous, too.
Middle school is gonna be the first time we don't have all our classes together.

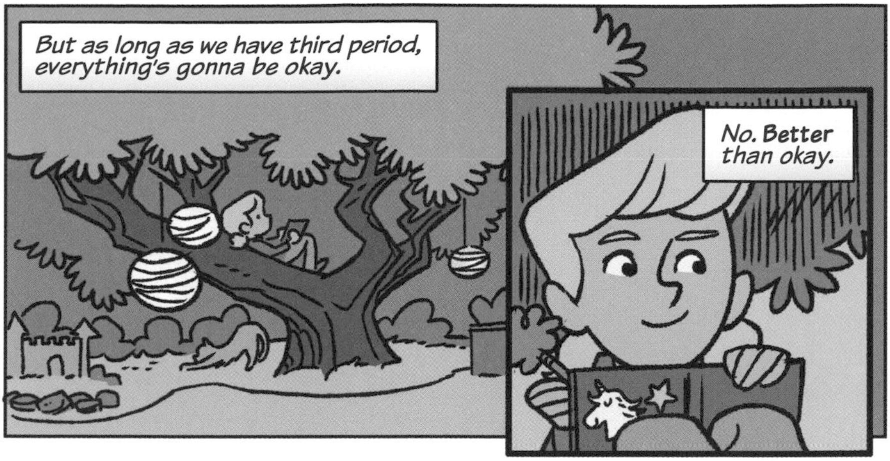
But as long as we have third period, everything's gonna be okay.
No. Better than okay.

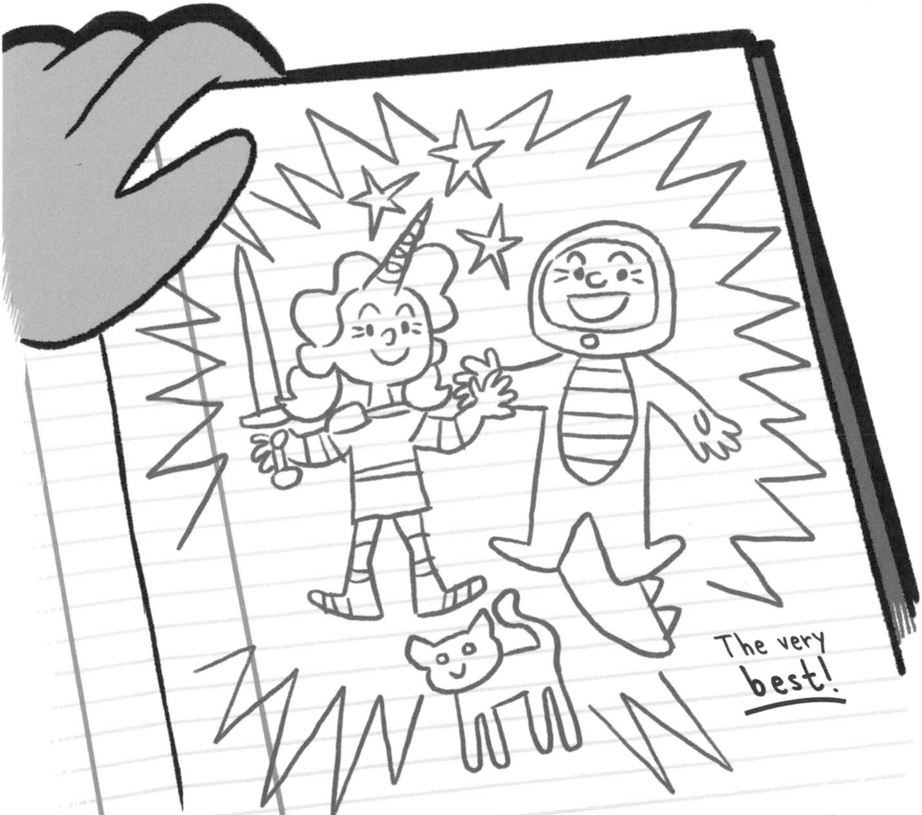
The very best!

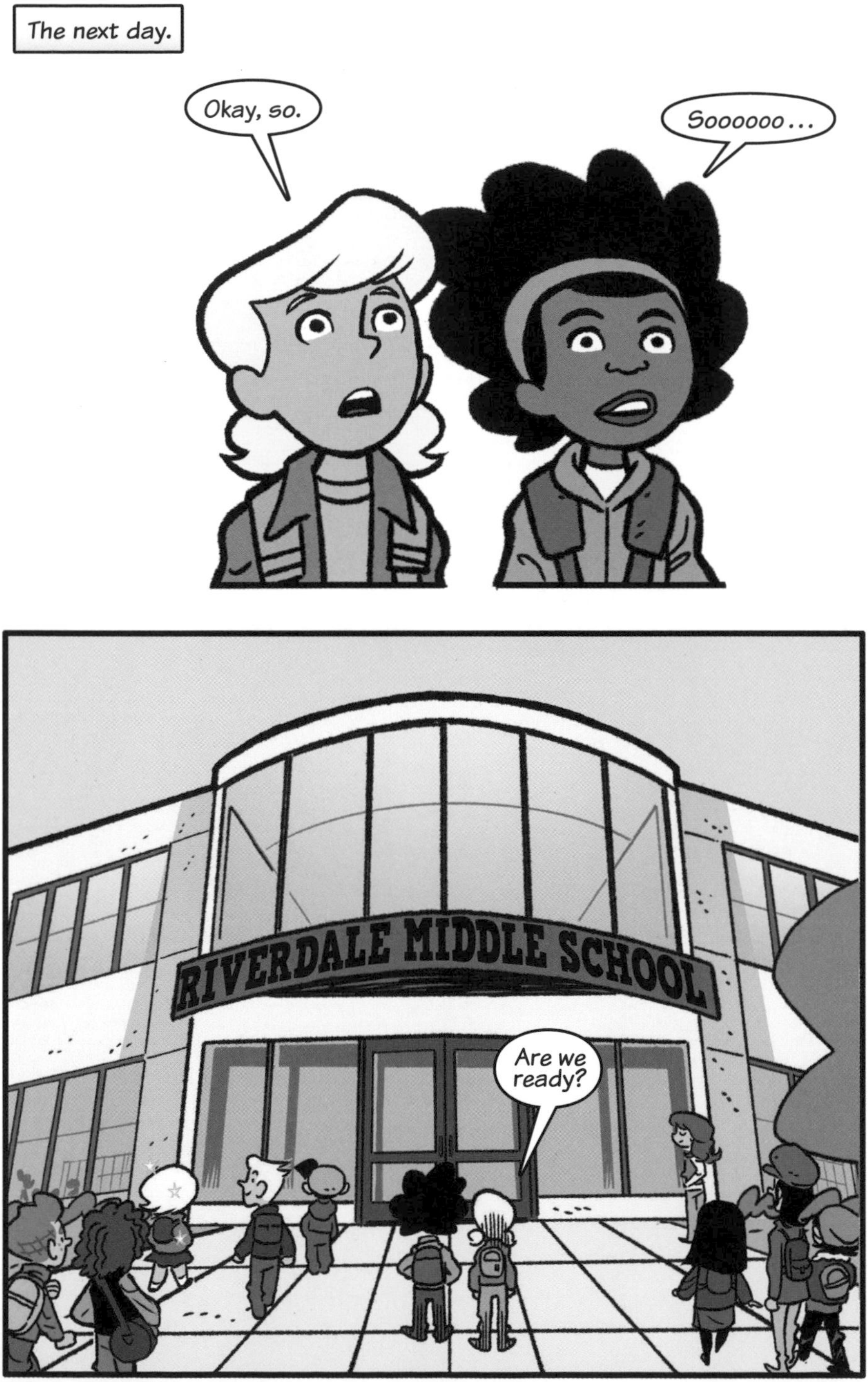
The next day.
Okay, so.
Sooooooo...
RIVERDALE MIDDLE SCHOOL
Are we ready?

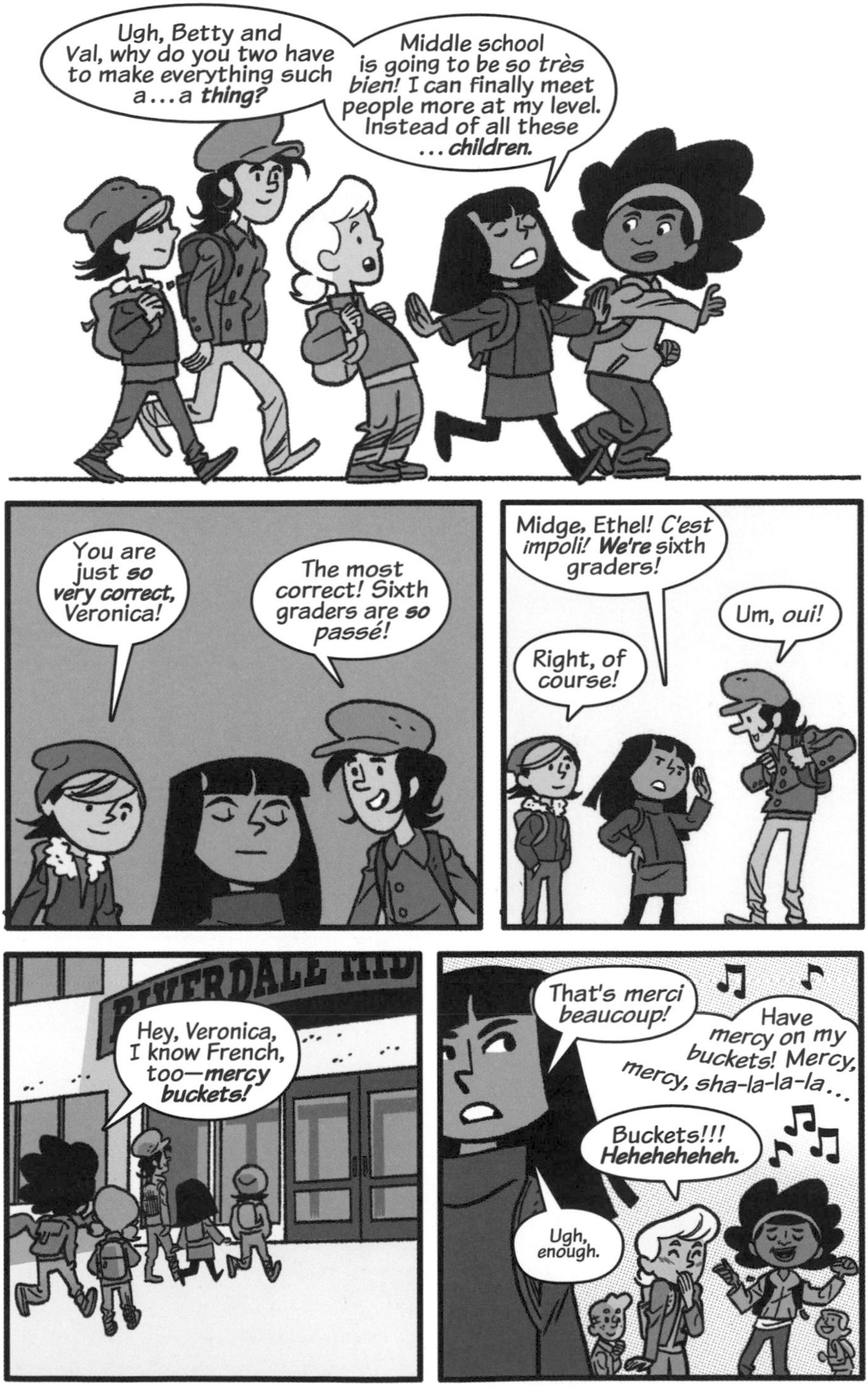
Ugh, Betty and Val, why do you two have to make everything such a...a *thing?*
Middle school is going to be so *très bien!* I can finally meet people more at my level. Instead of all these ...*children.*
You are just *so very correct,* Veronica!
The most correct! Sixth graders are *so passé!*
Midge, Ethel! *C'est impoli! We're* sixth graders!
Right, of course!
Um, *oui!*
RIVERDALE MID
Hey, Veronica, I know French, too—*mercy buckets!*
That's *merci beaucoup!*
Have *mercy* on my *buckets!* Mercy, mercy, sha-la-la-la...
Buckets!!! **Heheheheheh.**
Ugh, enough.

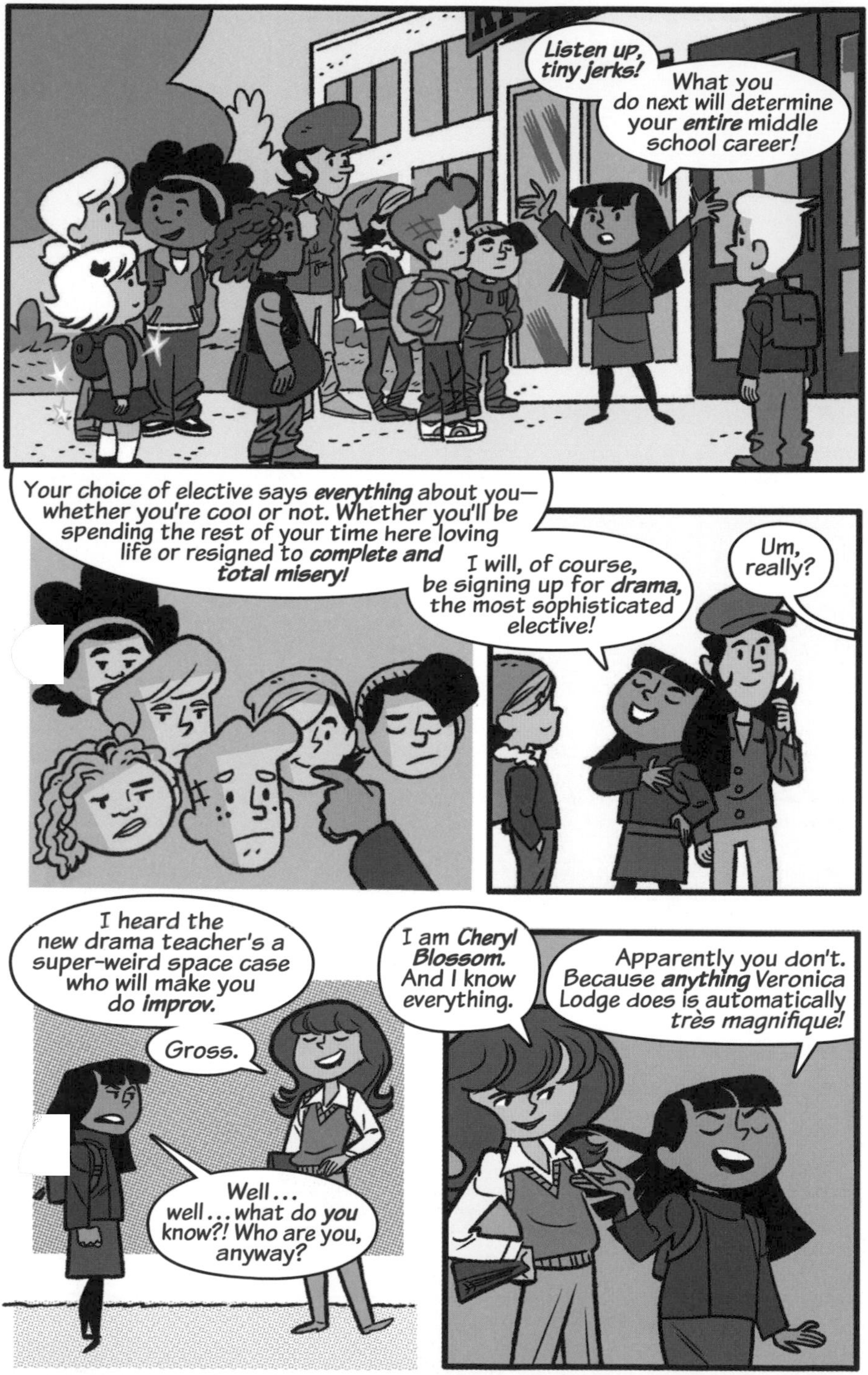

Listen up, tiny jerks!
What you do next will determine your *entire* middle school career!
Your choice of elective says *everything* about you—whether you're cool or not. Whether you'll be spending the rest of your time here loving life or resigned to *complete and total misery!*
I will, of course, be signing up for *drama,* the most sophisticated elective!
Um, really?
I heard the new drama teacher's a super-weird space case who will make you do *improv.*
Gross.
Well… well…what do *you* know?! Who are you, anyway?
I am *Cheryl Blossom.* And I know everything.
Apparently you don't. Because *anything* Veronica Lodge does is automatically *très magnifique!*

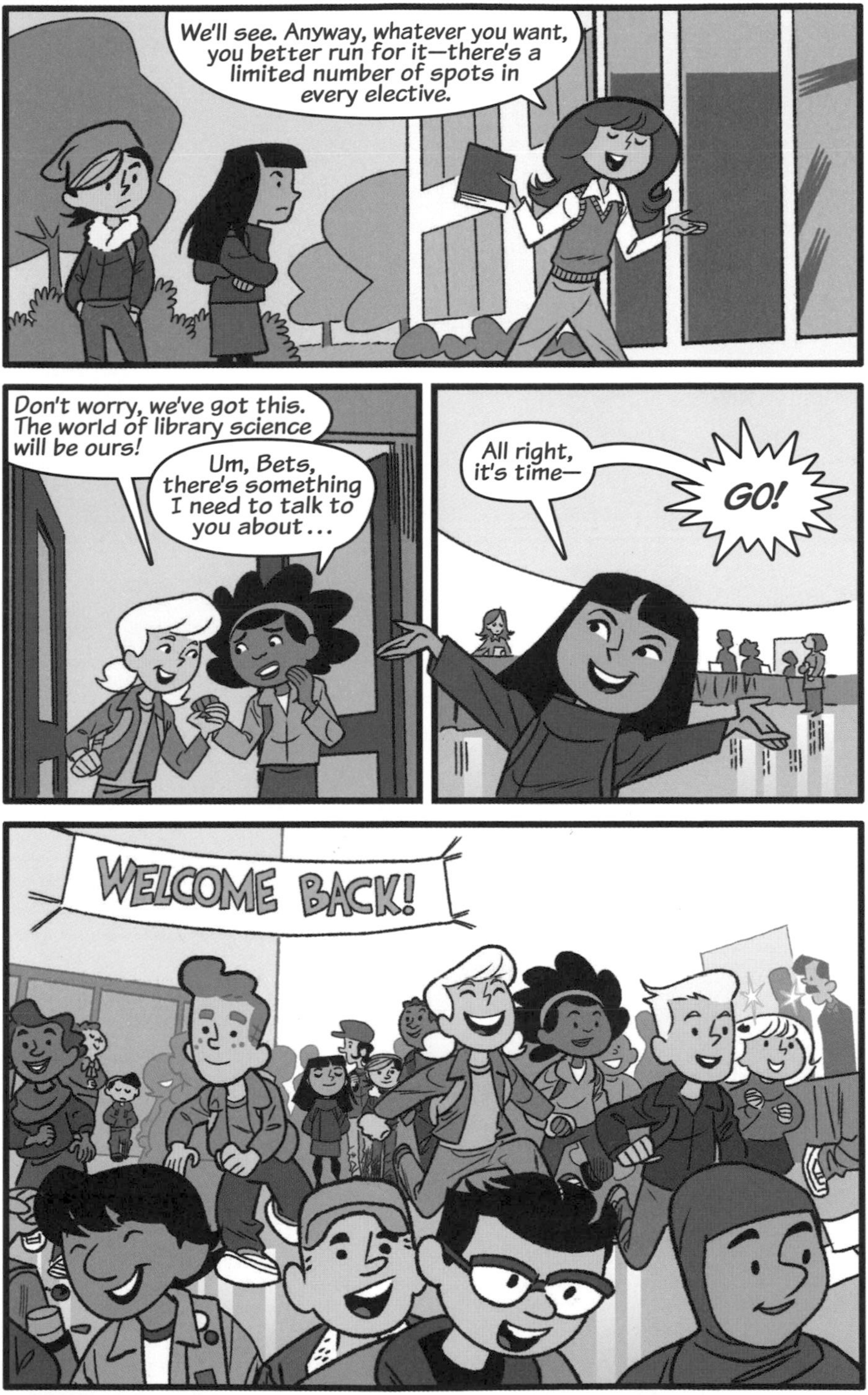
We'll see. Anyway, whatever you want, you better run for it—there's a limited number of spots in every elective.
Don't worry, we've got this. The world of library science will be ours!
Um, Bets, there's something I need to talk to you about...
All right, it's time—
GO!
WELCOME BACK!

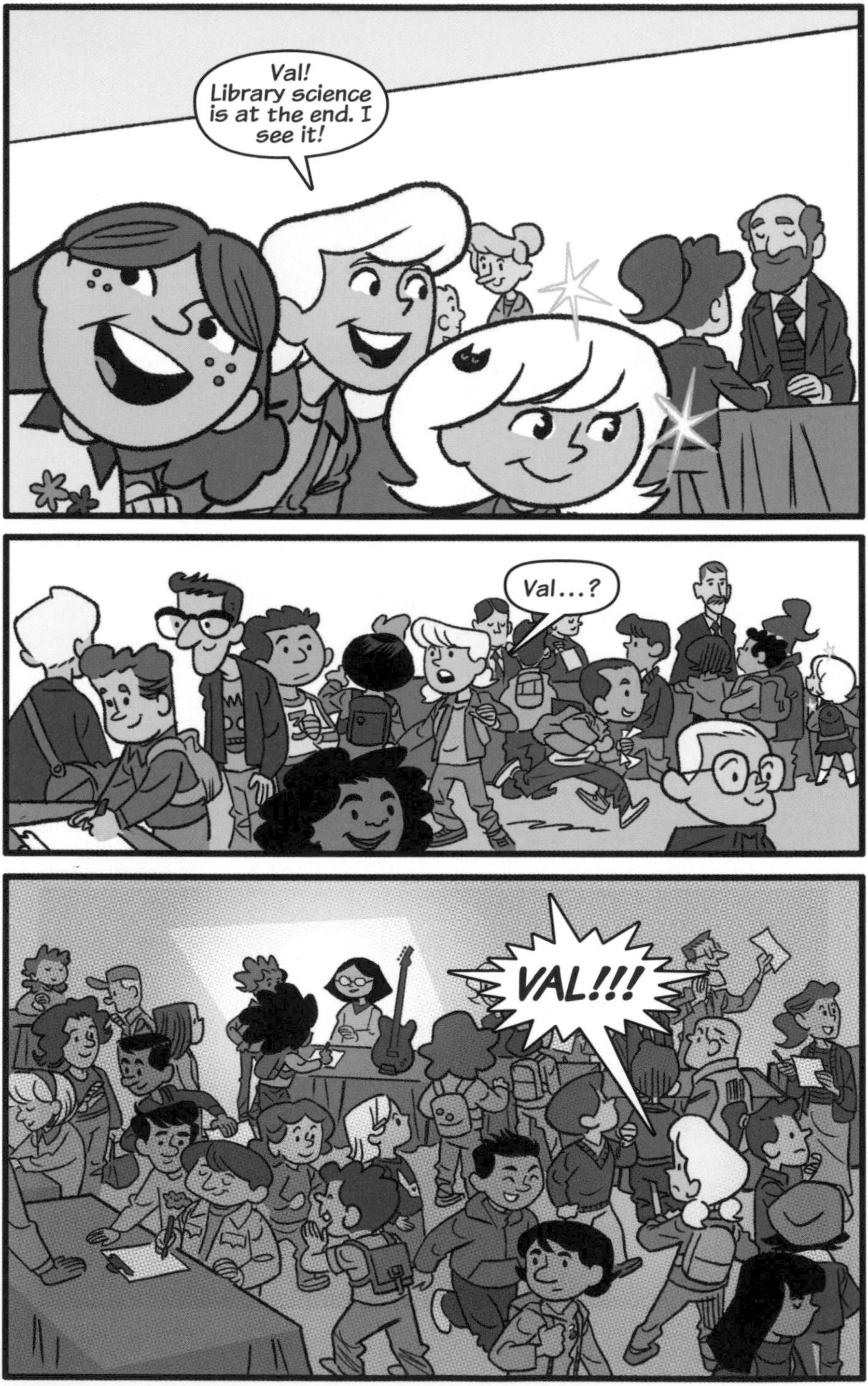
Val! Library science is at the end. I see it!
Val...?
VAL!!!

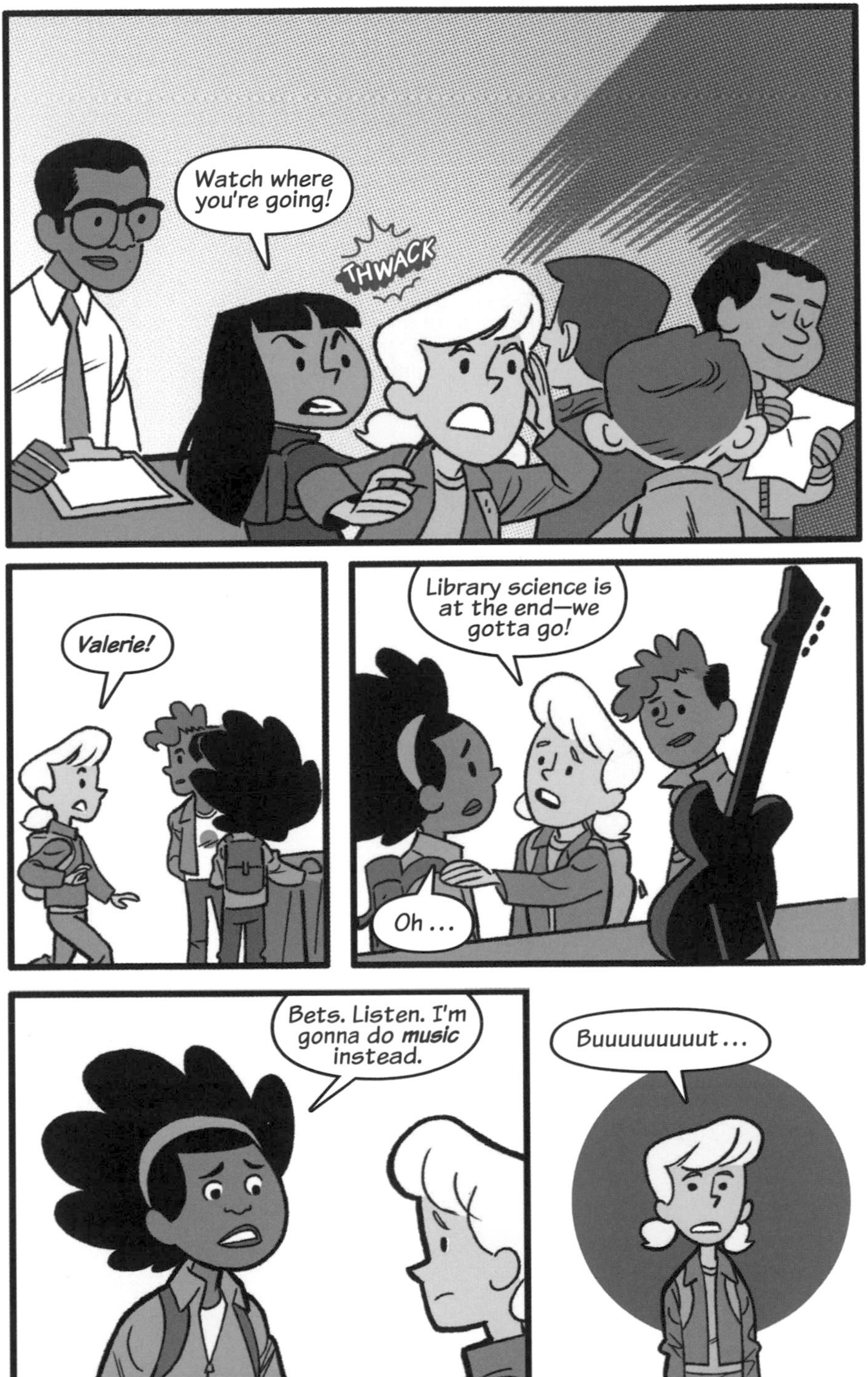
Watch where you're going!
THWACK
Valerie!
Library science is at the end—we gotta go!
Oh . . .
Bets. Listen. I'm gonna do *music* instead.
Buuuuuuuuut . . .

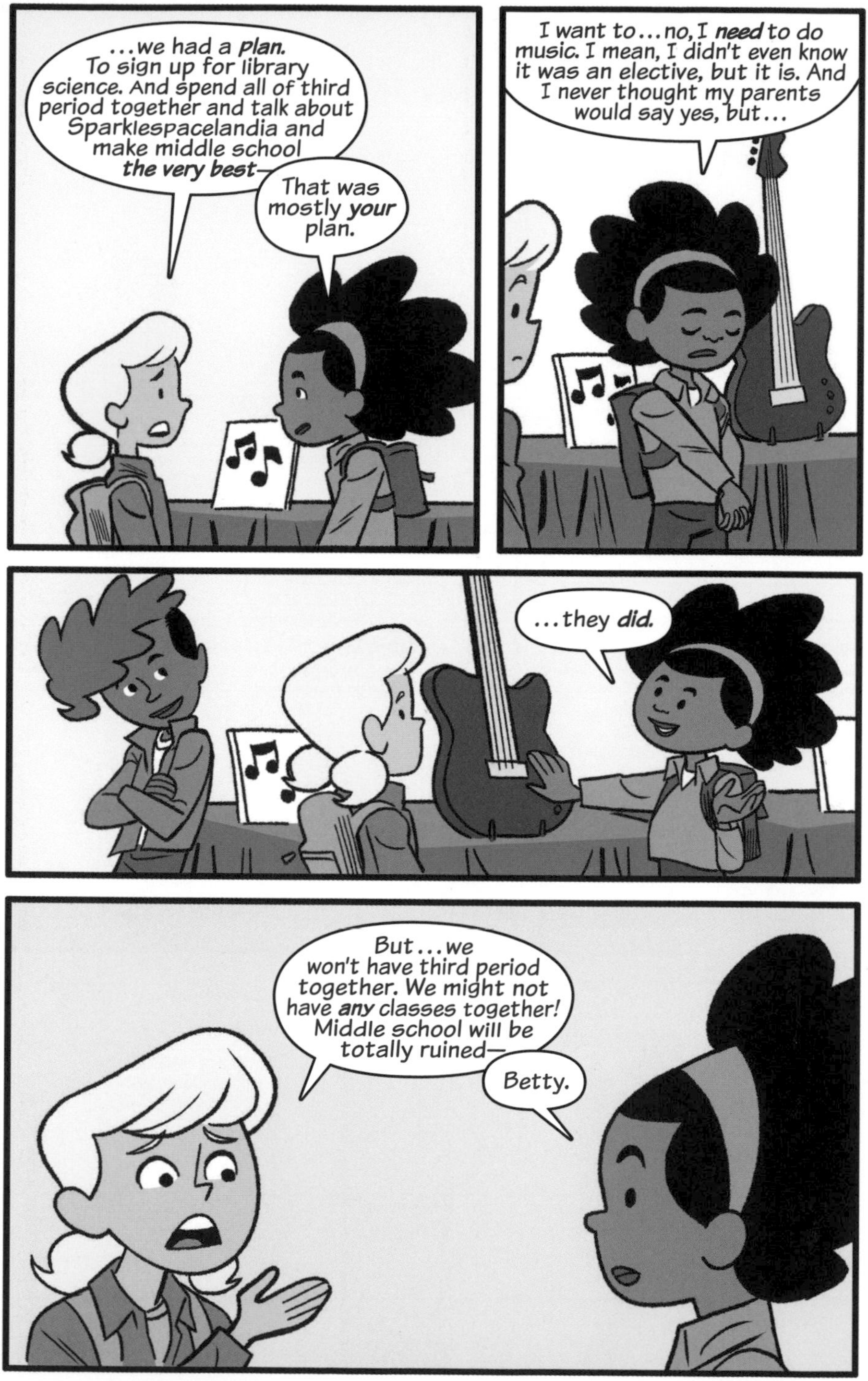
...we had a *plan.* To sign up for library science. And spend all of third period together and talk about Sparklespacelandia and make middle school ***the very best***—
That was mostly ***your*** plan.
I want to... no, I ***need*** to do music. I mean, I didn't even know it was an elective, but it is. And I never thought my parents would say yes, but...
...they ***did.***
But... we won't have third period together. We might not have ***any*** classes together! Middle school will be totally ruined—
Betty.

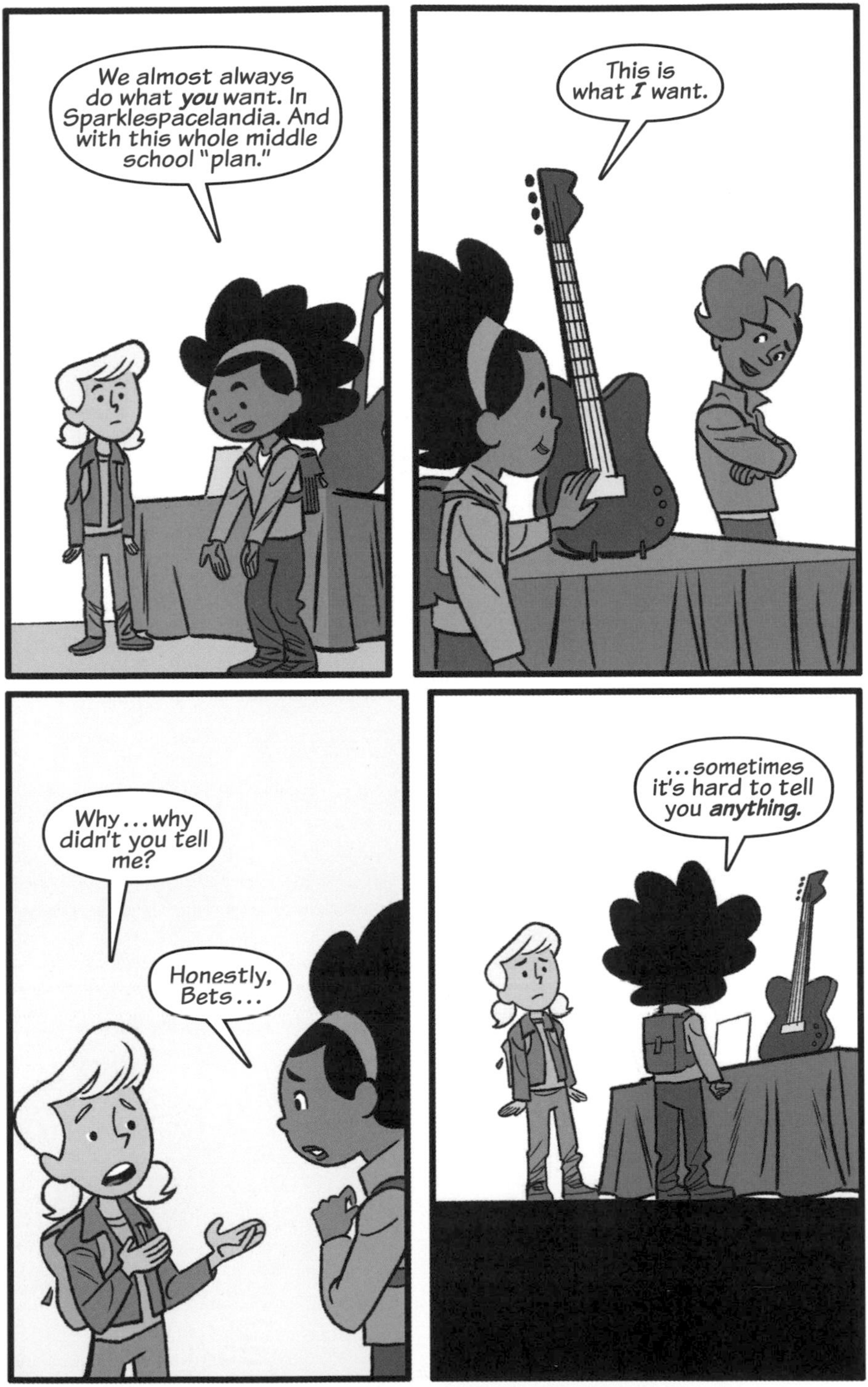
We almost always do what *you* want. In Sparklespacelandia. And with this whole middle school "plan."
This is what *I* want.
Why... why didn't you tell me?
Honestly, Bets...
...sometimes it's hard to tell you ***anything.***

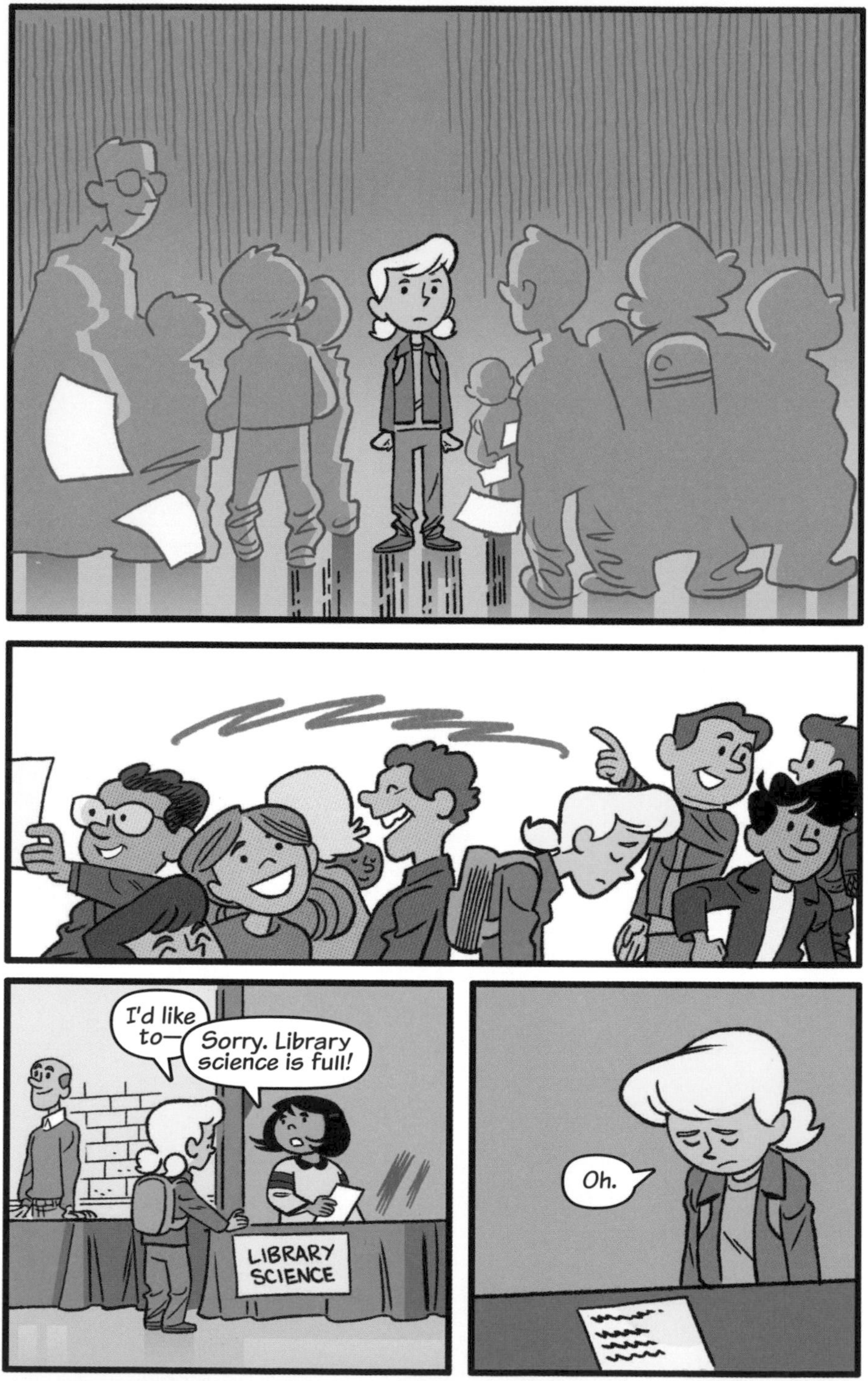
I'd like to—
Sorry. Library science is full!
LIBRARY SCIENCE
Oh.

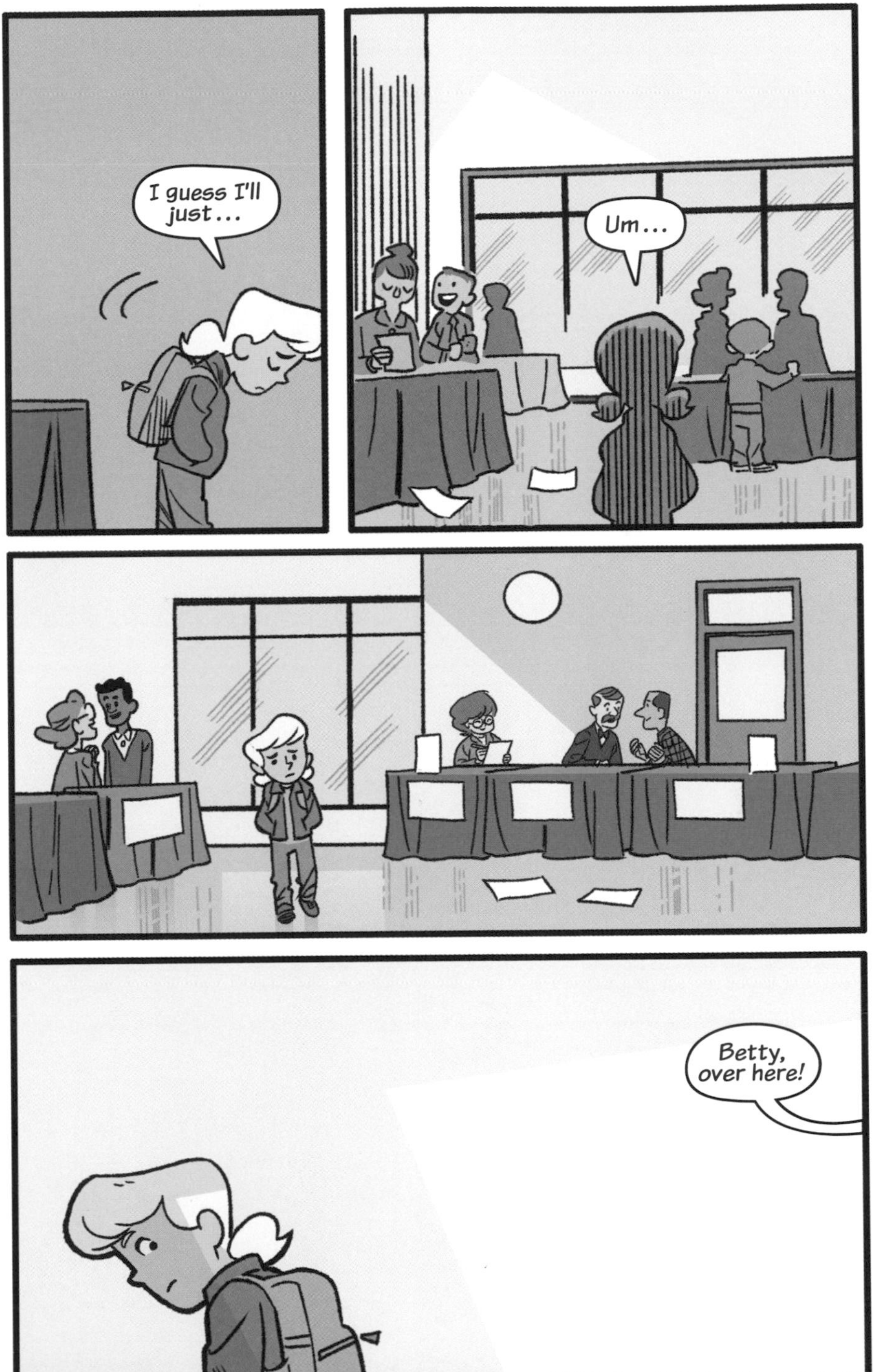
I guess I'll just...
Um...
Betty, over here!

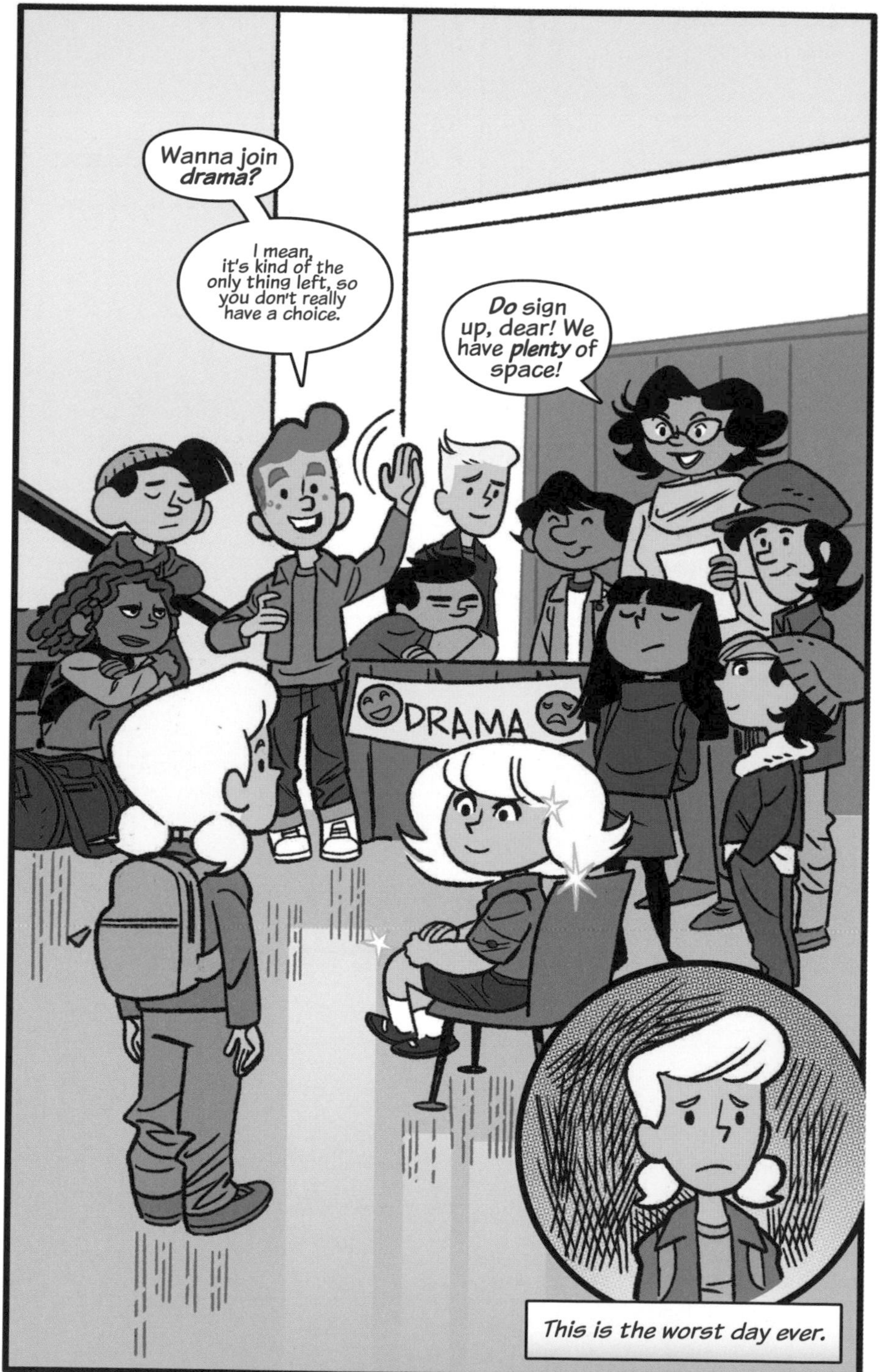
Wanna join drama?
I mean, it's kind of the only thing left, so you don't really have a choice.
Do sign up, dear! We have plenty of space!
DRAMA
This is the worst day ever.

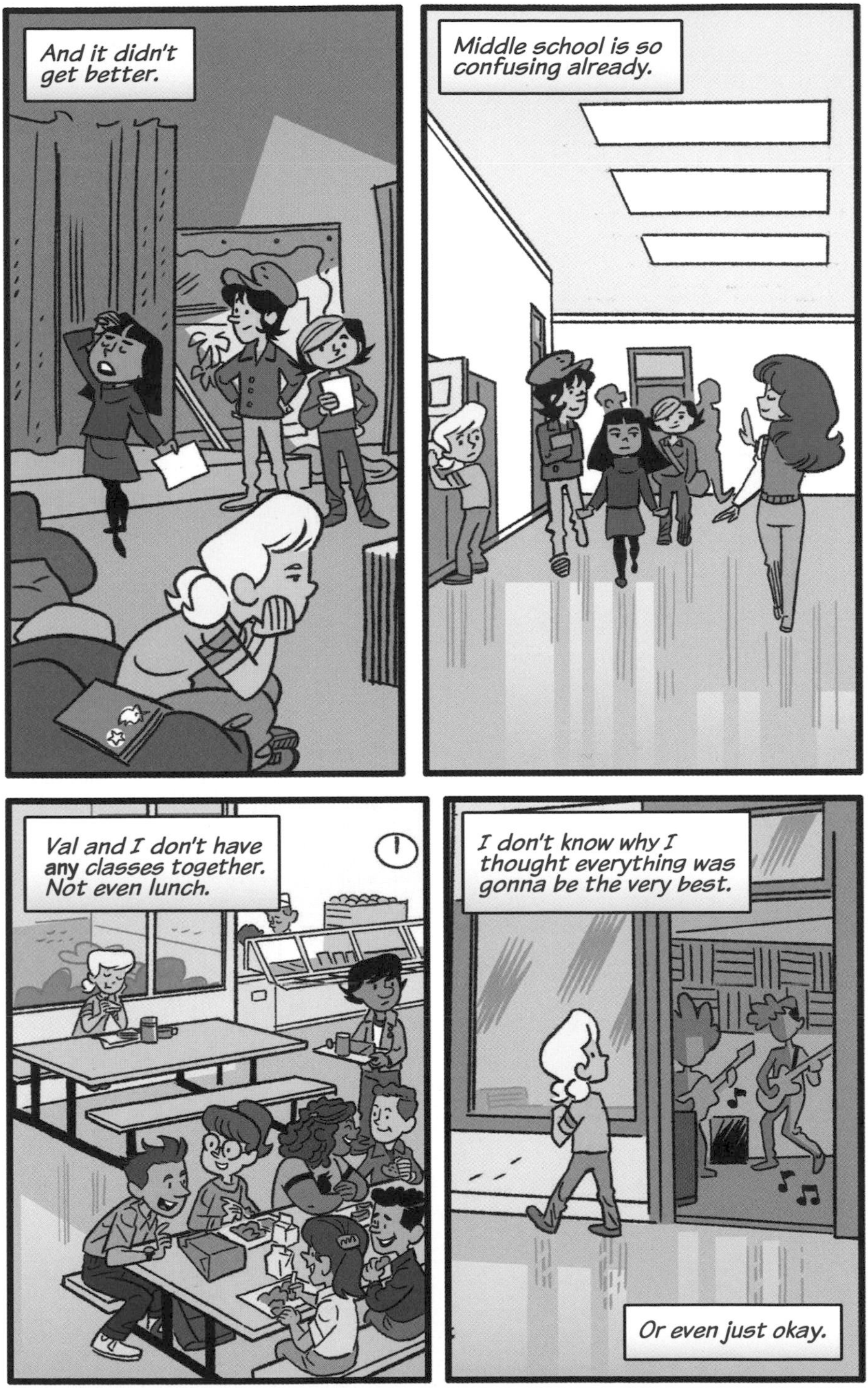
And it didn't get better.
Middle school is so confusing already.
Val and I don't have **any** classes together. Not even lunch.
I don't know why I thought everything was gonna be the very best.
Or even just okay.

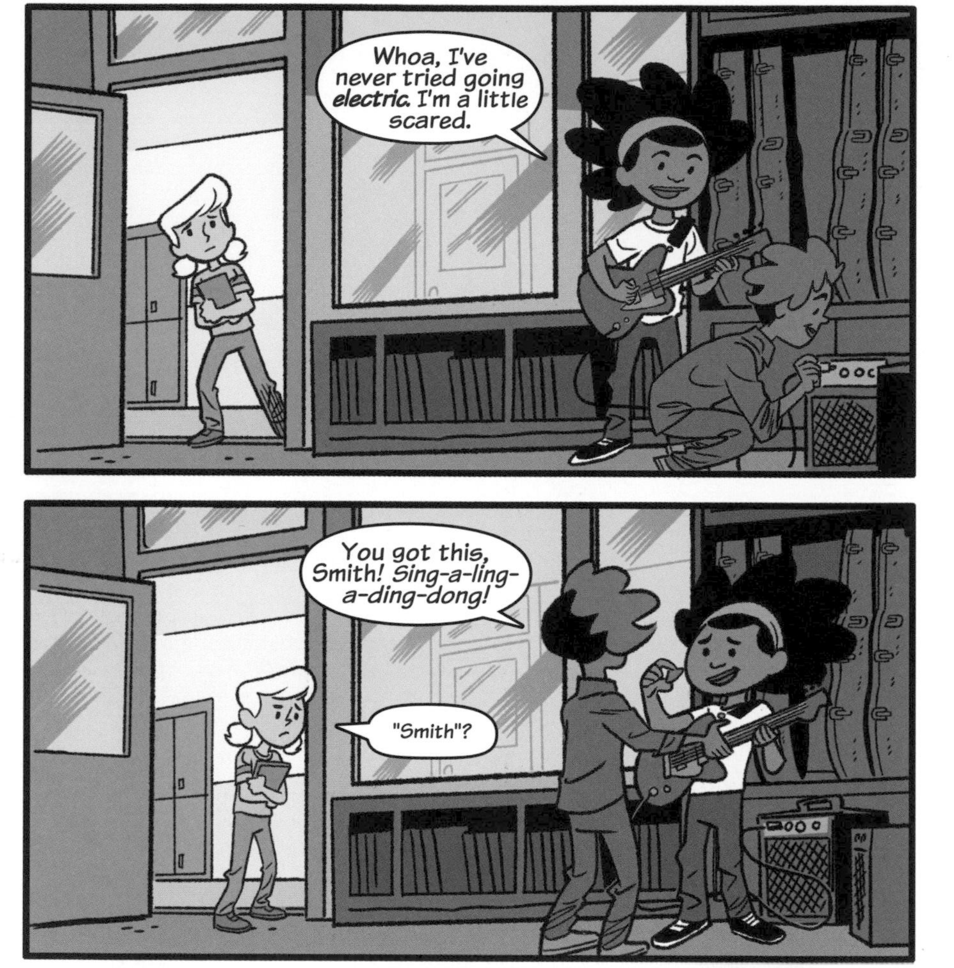
Whoa, I've never tried going *electric.* I'm a little scared.
You got this, Smith! *Sing-a-ling-a-ding-dong!*
"Smith"?
BWANG

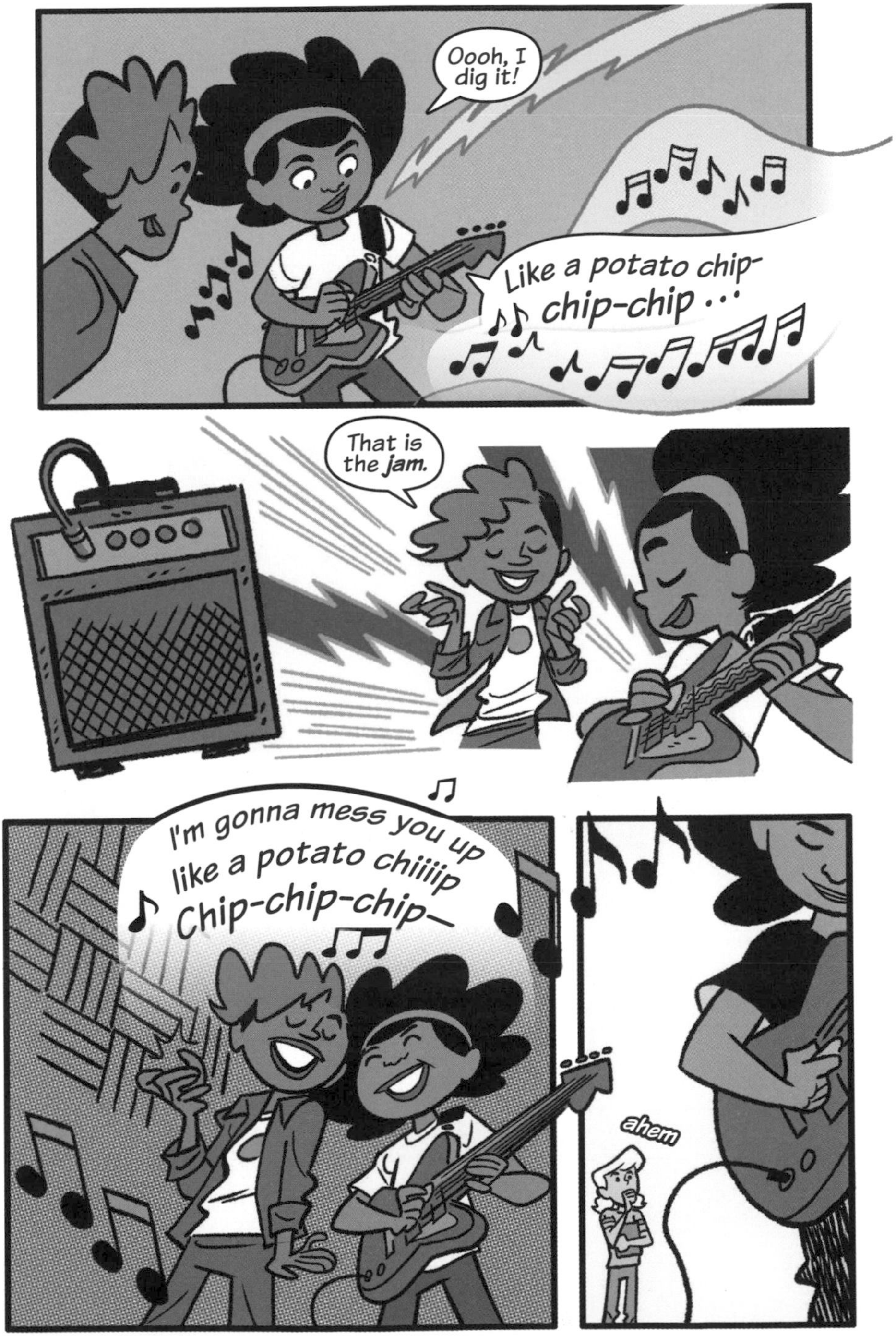
Oooh, I dig it!
Like a potato chip-chip-chip . . .
That is the *jam.*
I'm gonna mess you up like a potato chiiiip Chip-chip-chip—
ahem

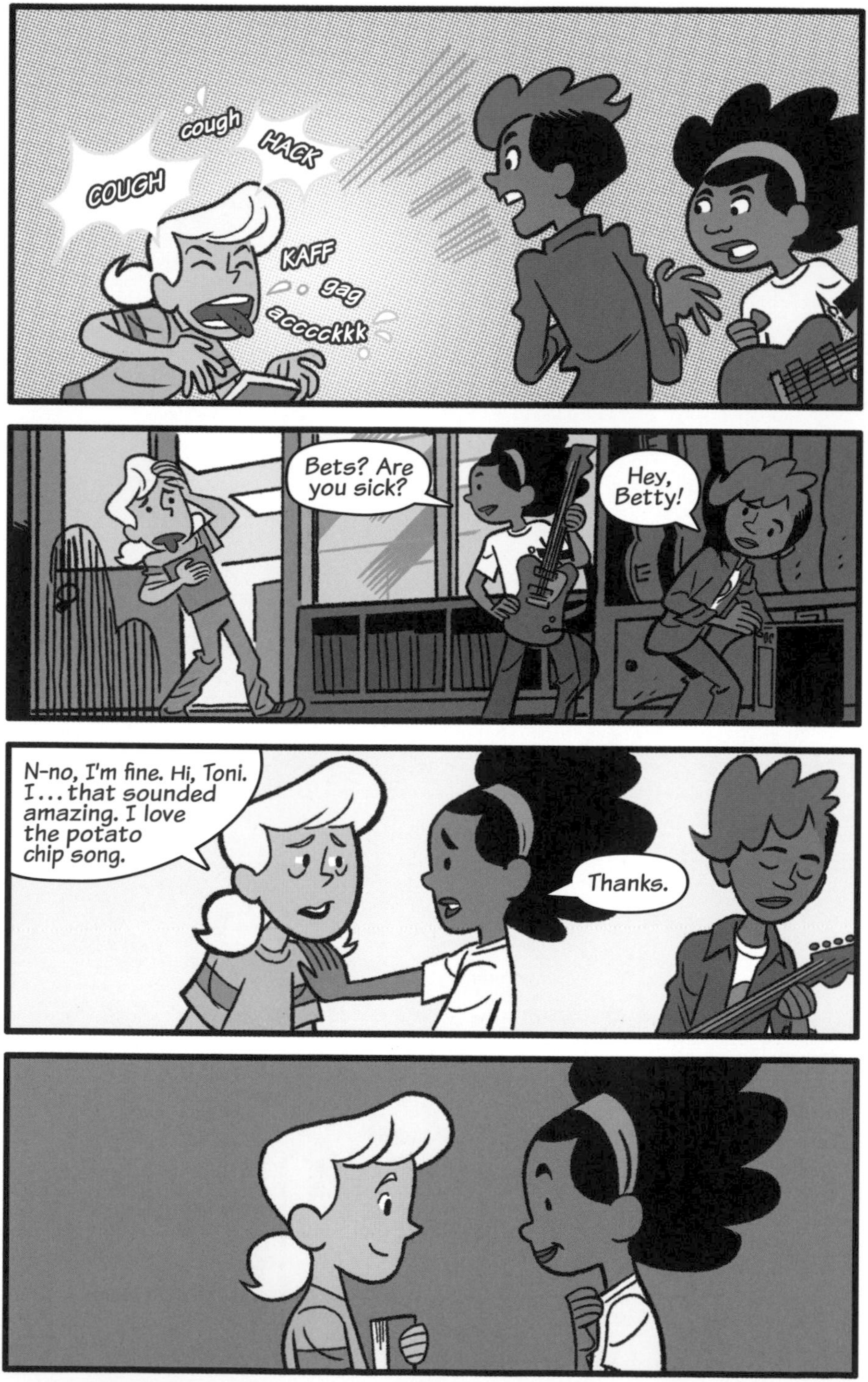
cough
HACK
COUGH
KAFF
gag
accccckkk
Bets? Are you sick?
Hey, Betty!
N-no, I'm fine. Hi, Toni. I... that sounded amazing. I love the potato chip song.
Thanks.

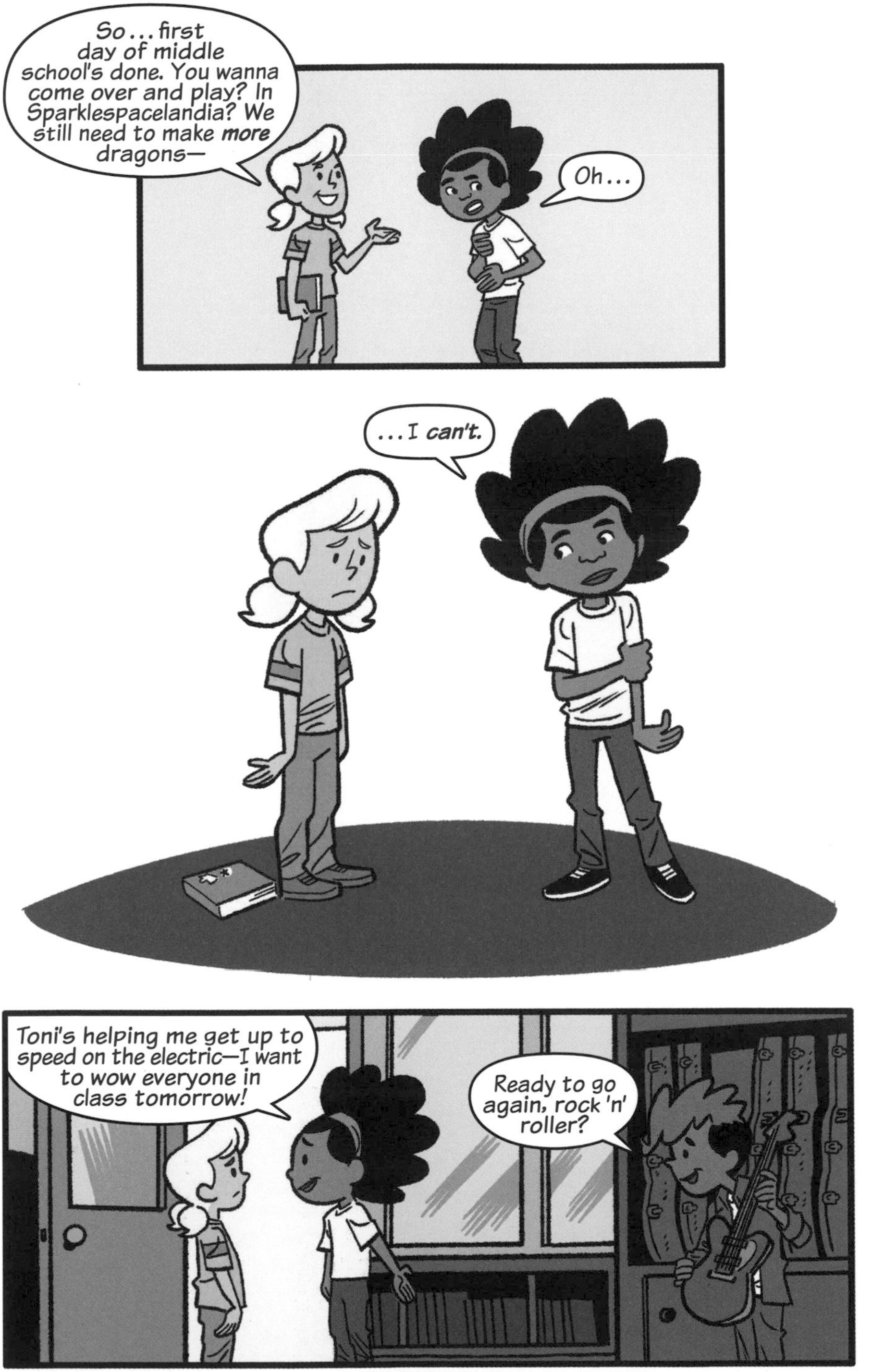
So... first day of middle school's done. You wanna come over and play? In Sparklespacelandia? We still need to make *more* dragons—
Oh...
...I *can't.*
Toni's helping me get up to speed on the electric—I want to wow everyone in class tomorrow!
Ready to go again, rock 'n' roller?

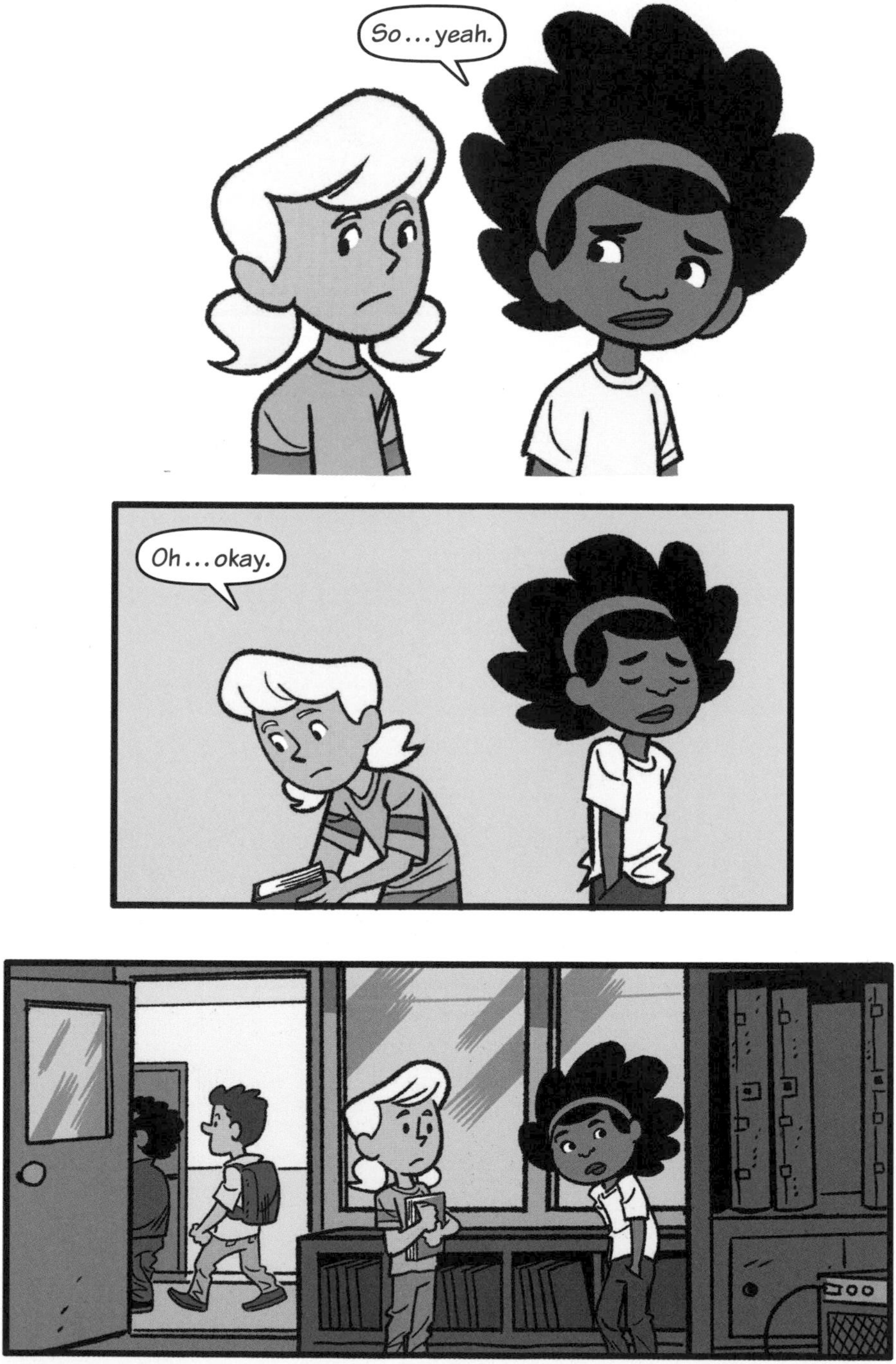
So... yeah.
Oh... okay.

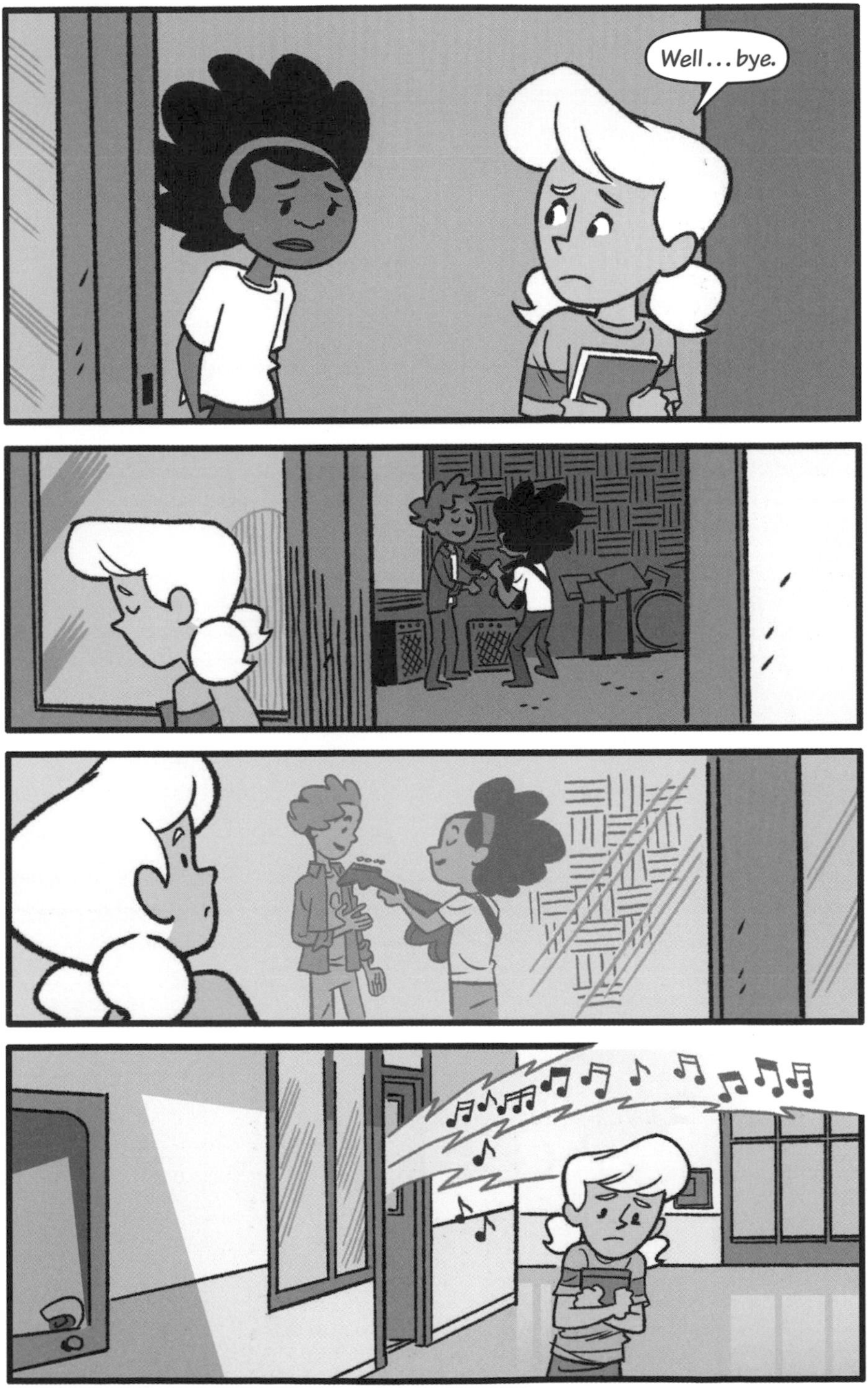
Well . . . bye.

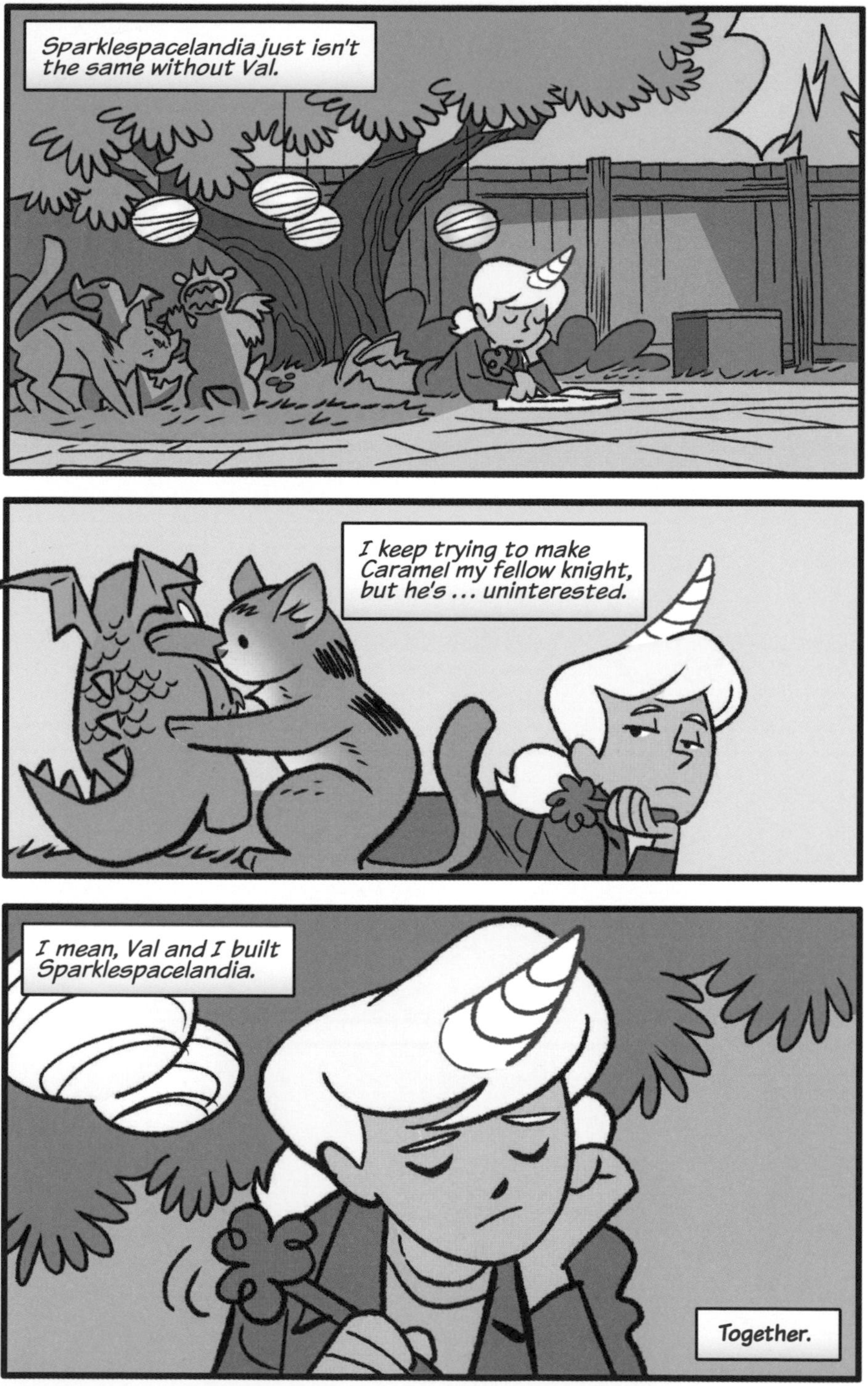
Sparklespacelandia just isn't the same without Val.
I keep trying to make Caramel my fellow knight, but he's ... uninterested.
I mean, Val and I built Sparklespacelandia.
Together.

33

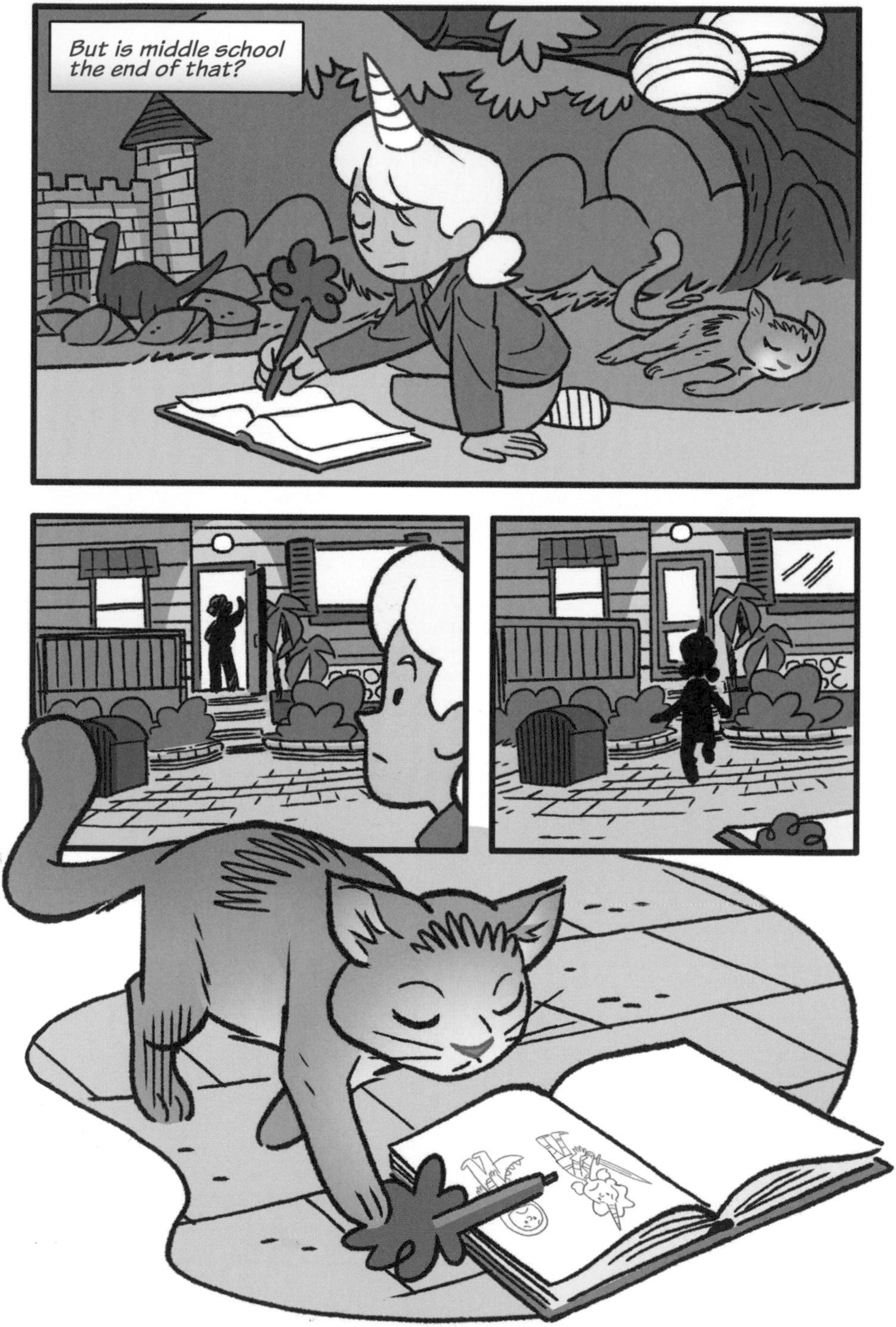
But is middle school the end of that?

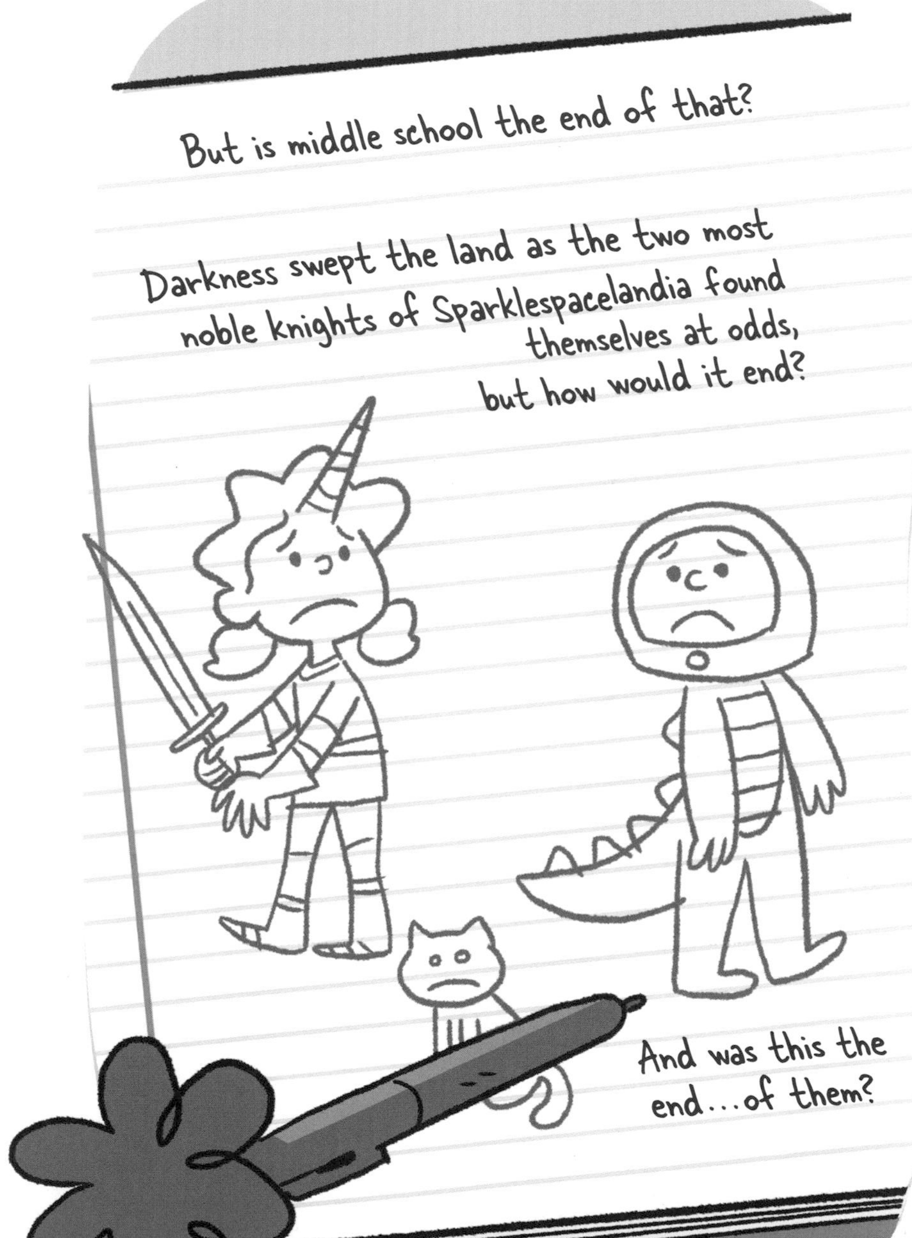
But is middle school the end of that?
Darkness swept the land as the two most noble knights of Sparklespacelandia found themselves at odds, but how would it end?
And was this the end...of them?

36

37

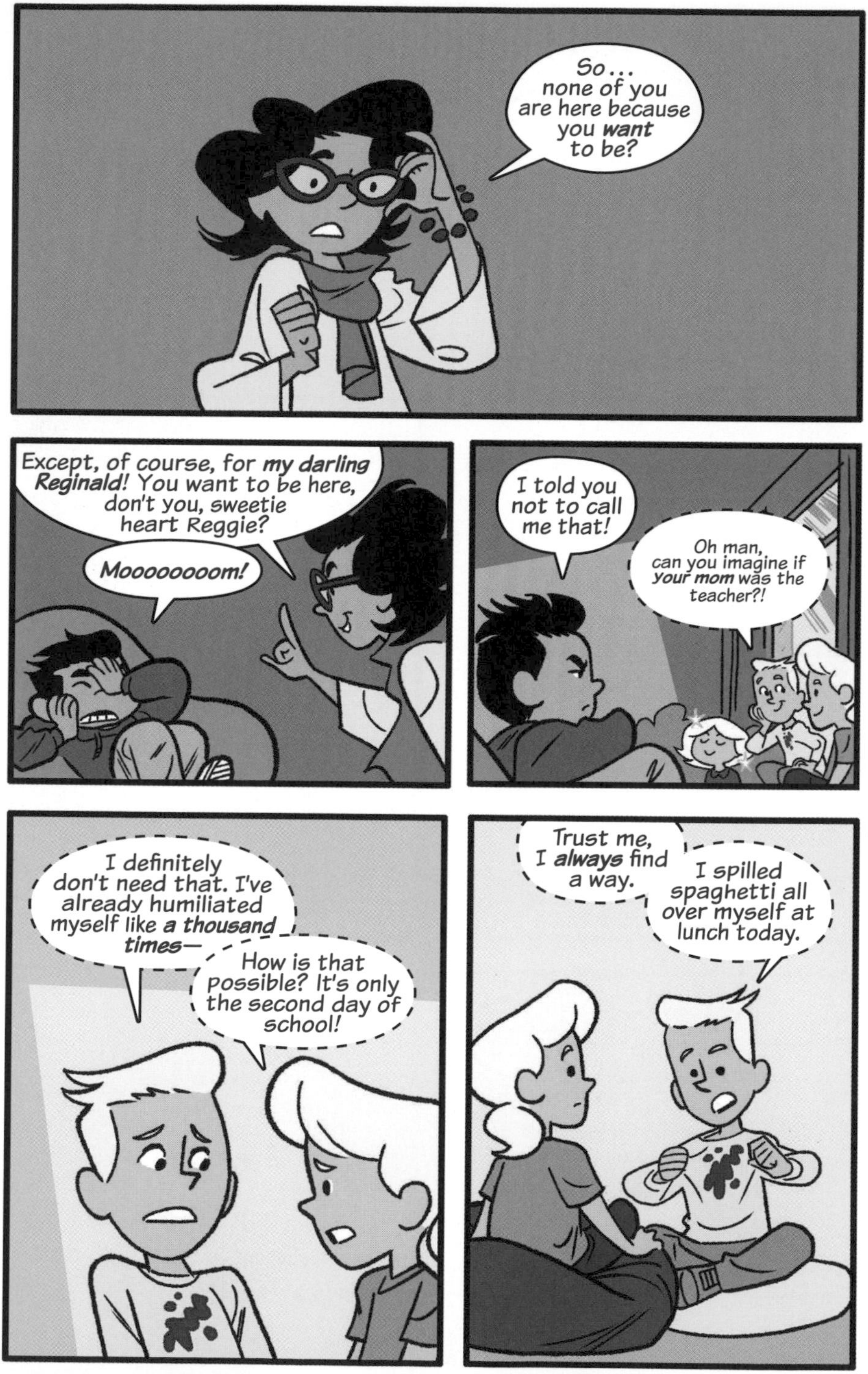
So... none of you are here because you **want** to be?
Except, of course, for **my darling Reginald**! You want to be here, don't you, sweetie heart Reggie?
Mooooooooom!
I told you not to call me that!
Oh man, can you imagine if **your mom** was the teacher?!
I definitely don't need that. I've already humiliated myself like **a thousand times**—
How is that possible? It's only the second day of school!
Trust me, I **always** find a way.
I spilled spaghetti all over myself at lunch today.

40

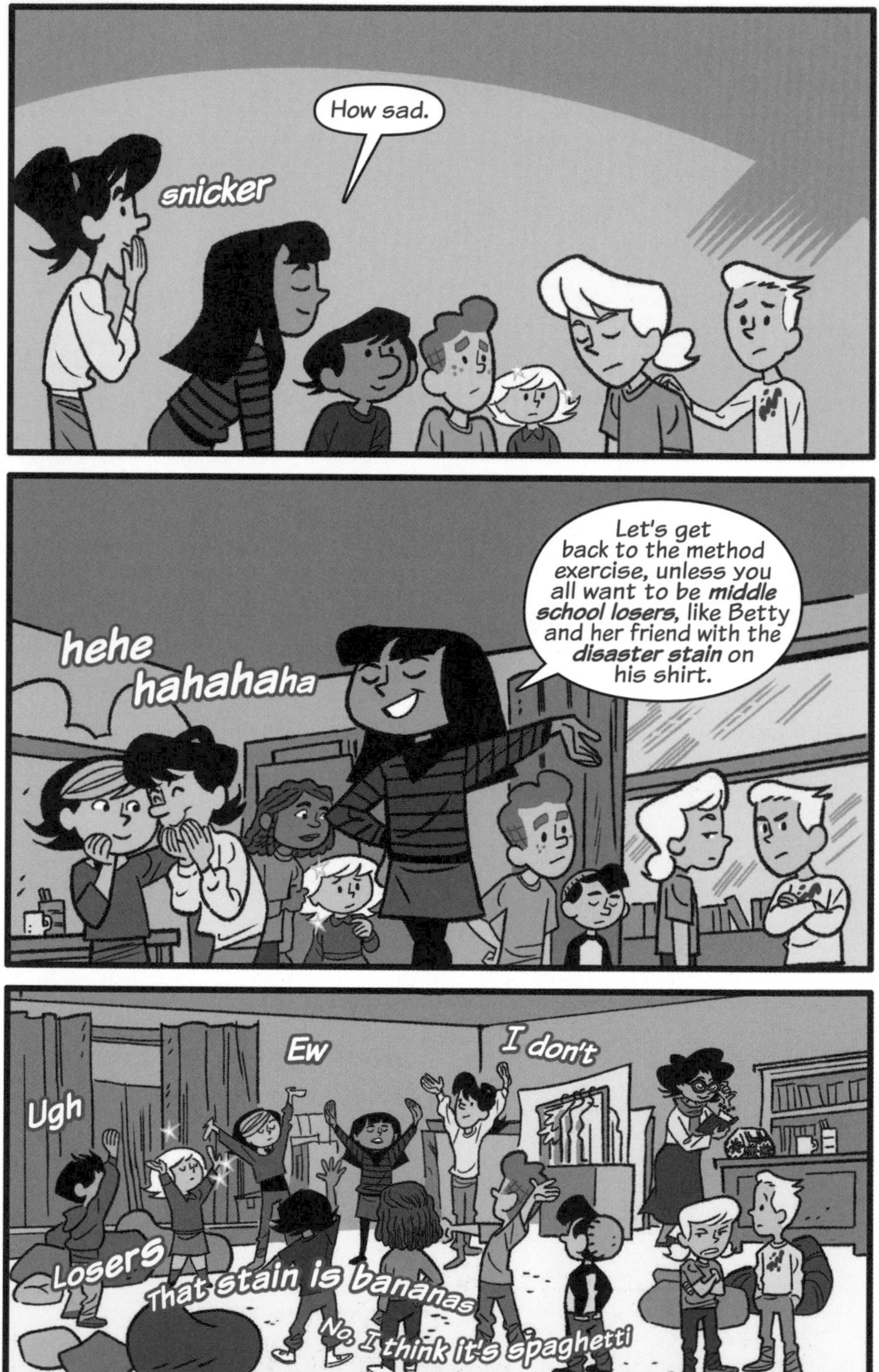
How sad.
snicker
Let's get back to the method exercise, unless you all want to be *middle school losers,* like Betty and her friend with the *disaster stain* on his shirt.
hehe
hahahahaha
Ugh
Ew
I don't
Losers
That stain is bananas
No, I think it's spaghetti

43

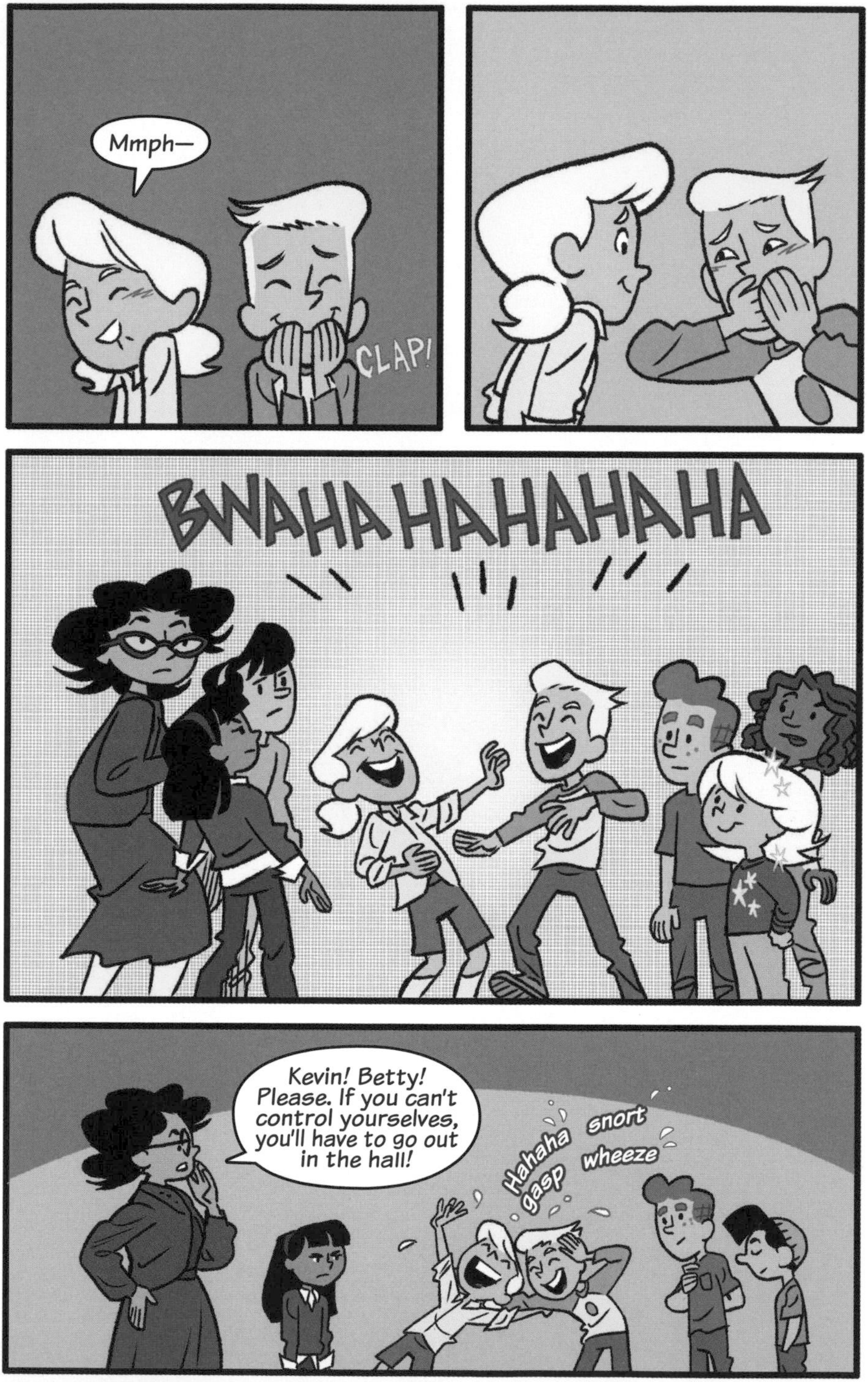

Mmph—
CLAP!
BWAHAHAHAHAHAHA
Kevin! Betty! Please. If you can't control yourselves, you'll have to go out in the hall!
Hahaha snort
gasp wheeze

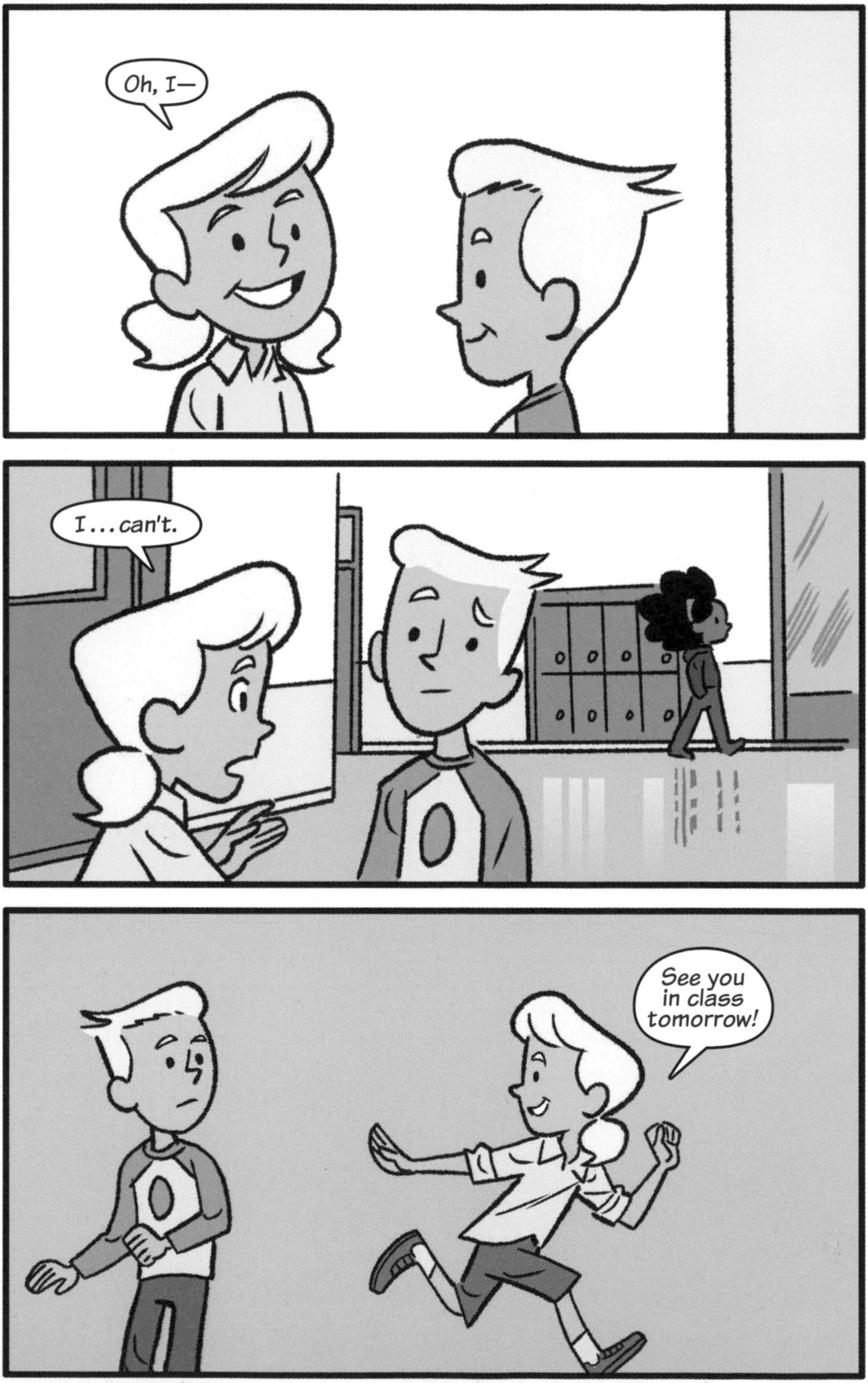
Oh, I—
I...can't.
See you in class tomorrow!

47

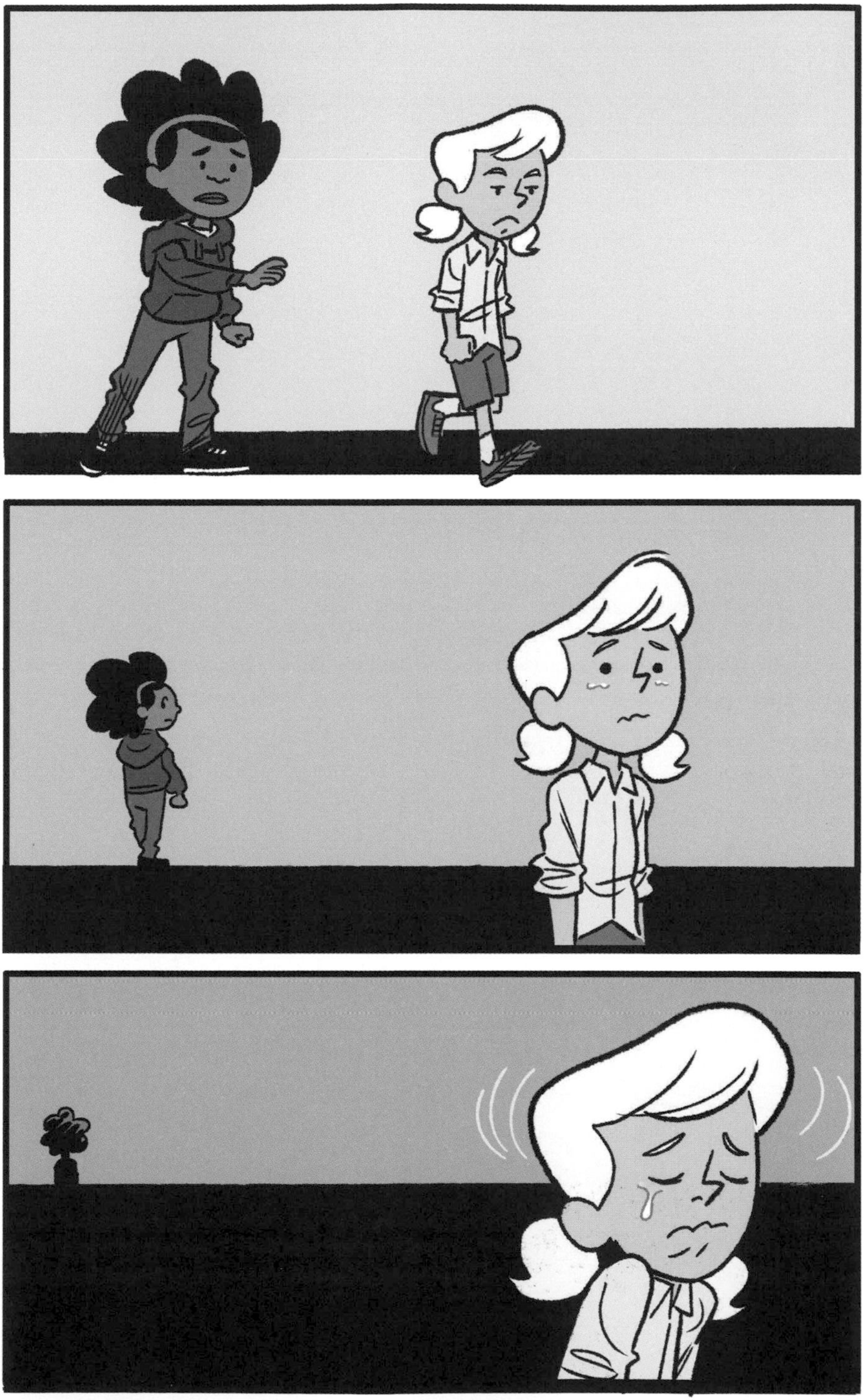

50

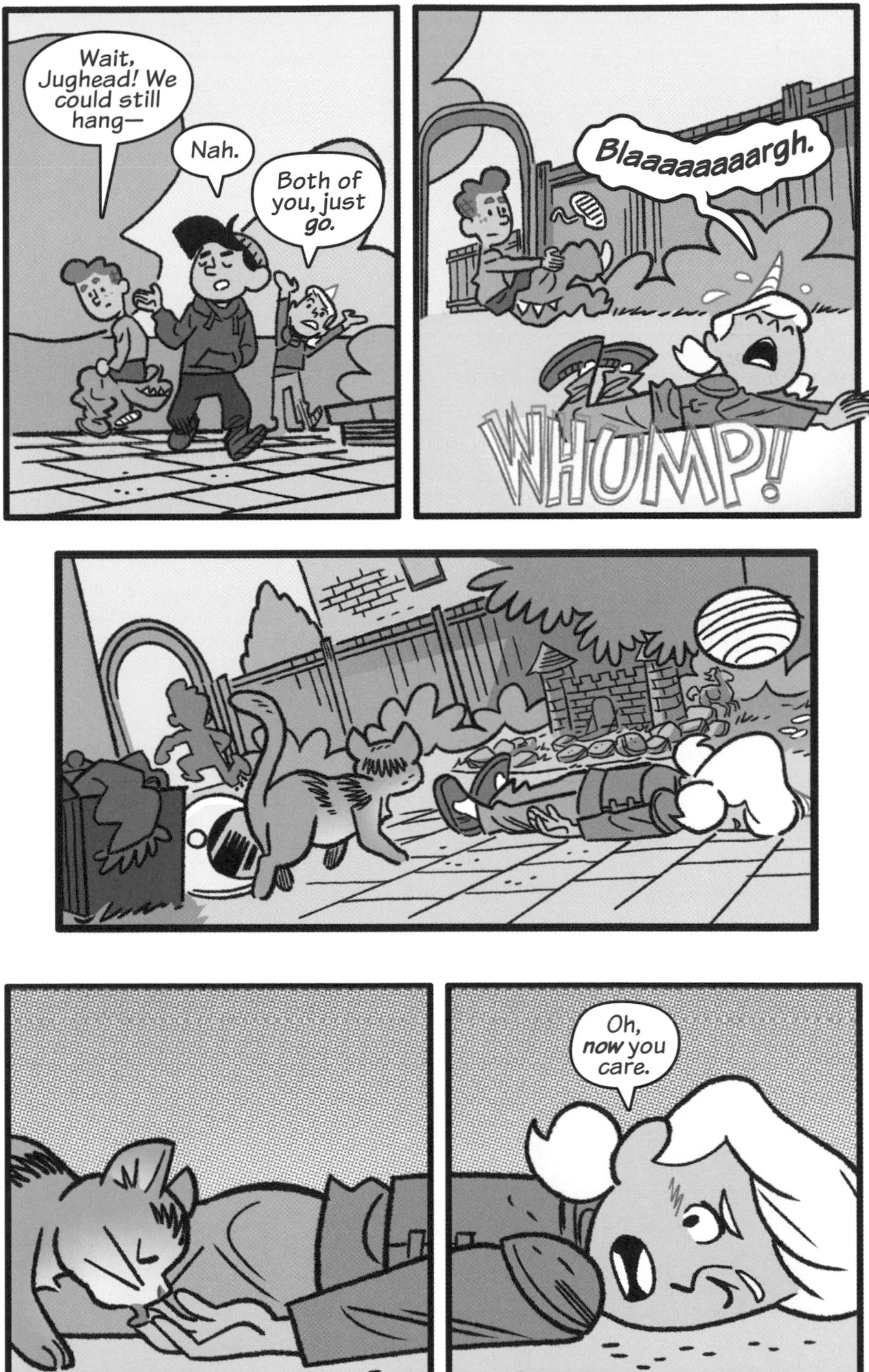
Wait, Jughead! We could still hang—
Nah.
Both of you, just *go.*
Blaaaaaaaargh.
WHUMP!
Oh, *now* you care.

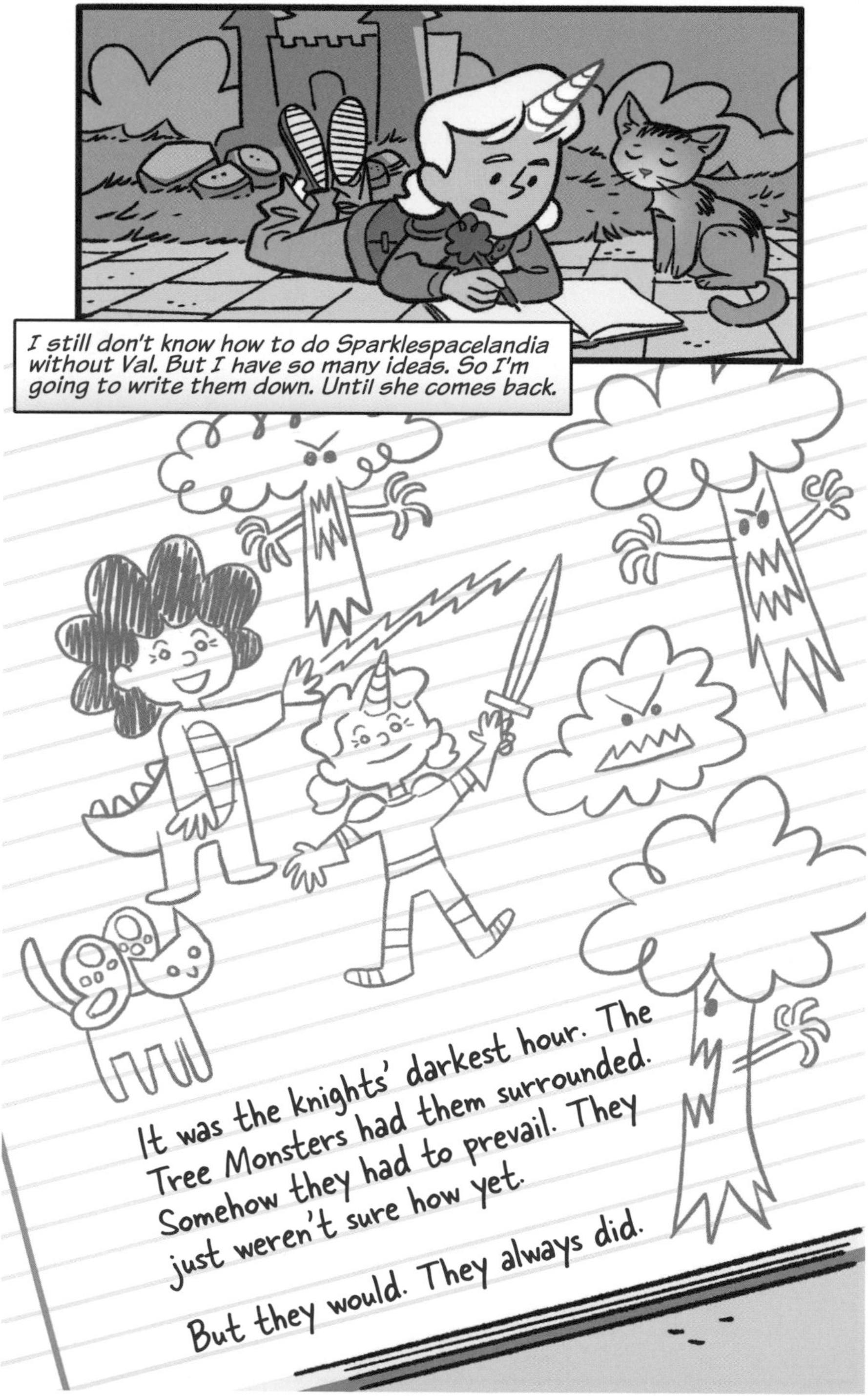
I still don't know how to do Sparklespacelandia without Val. But I have so many ideas. So I'm going to write them down. Until she comes back.
It was the knights' darkest hour. The Tree Monsters had them surrounded. Somehow they had to prevail. They just weren't sure how yet.
But they would. They always did.

It's been a month and middle school is still confusing.

Val's still busy with music stuff every day after school.

But I'm working hard on all my ideas for Sparklespacelandia, so they'll be ready whenever she comes back.

Little thespians, we are still perfecting the tree exercise. Today's outdoor classroom is meant to make you feel truly at one with the trees! Take it all in!

Come on, my sweetie heart Reggie! *Be the tree!* Find that creative spark I know exists within—

Ugh, drama losers.

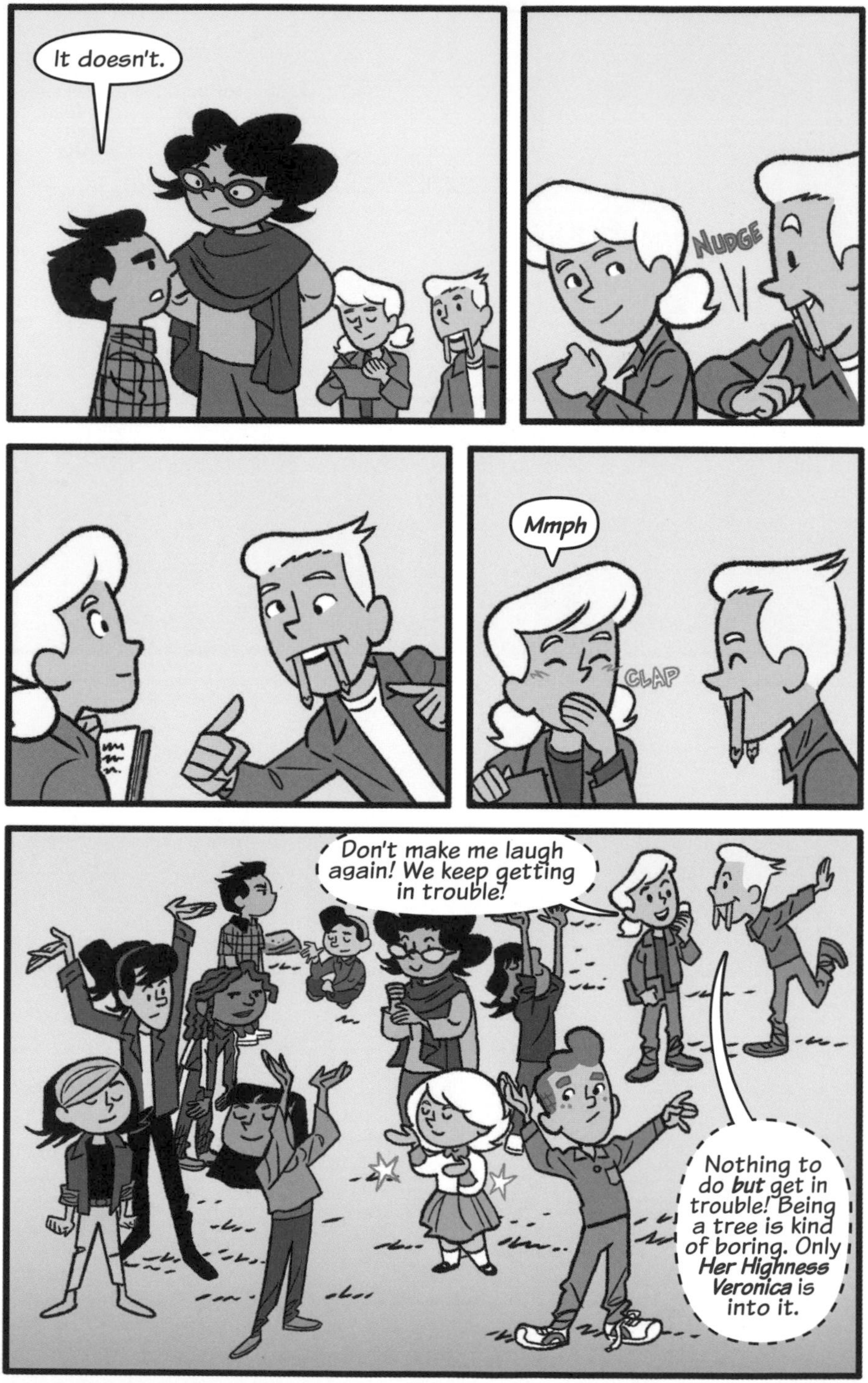
It doesn't.
NUDGE
Mmph
CLAP
Don't make me laugh again! We keep getting in trouble!
Nothing to do **but** get in trouble! Being a tree is kind of boring. Only ***Her Highness Veronica*** is into it.

56

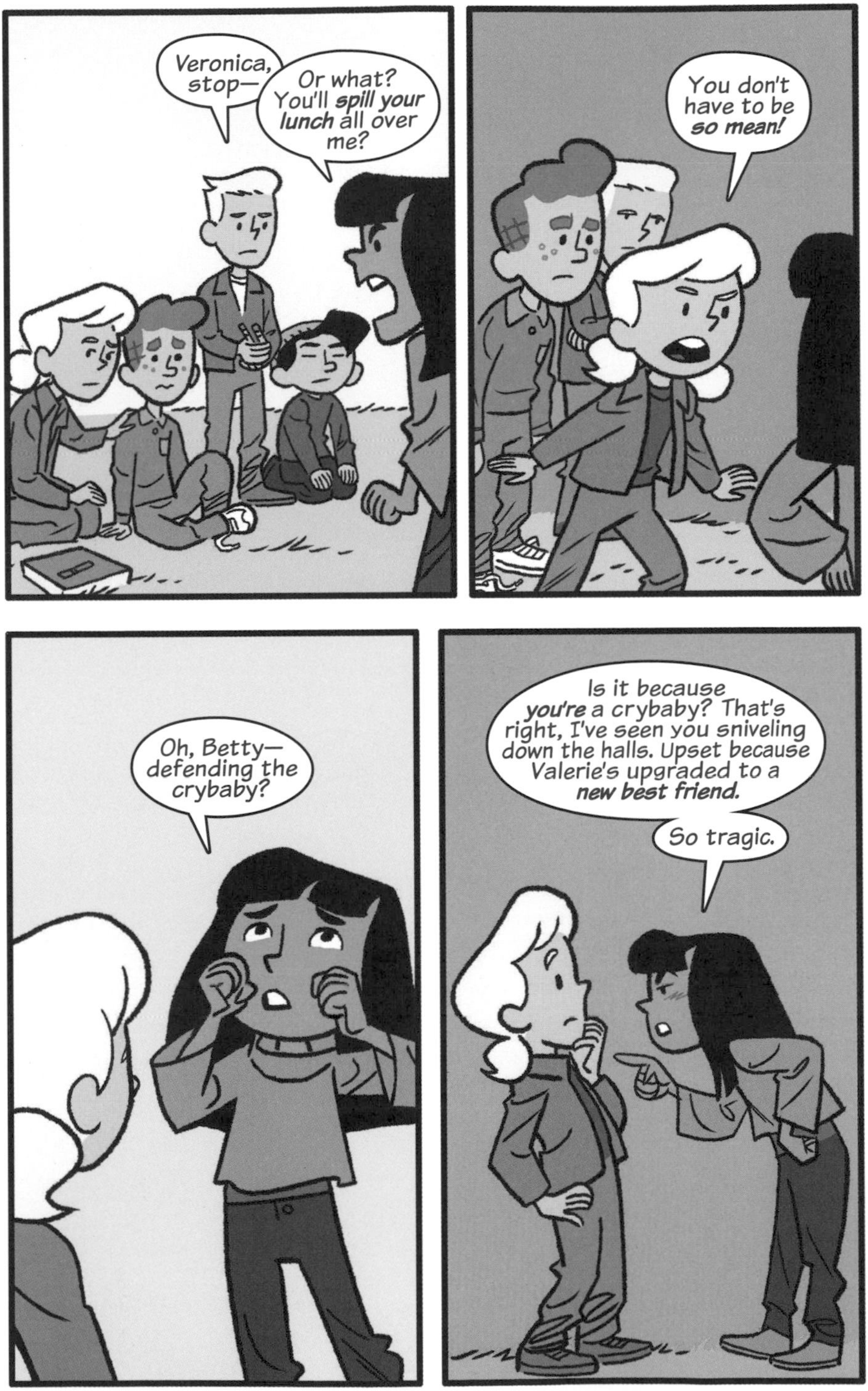
Veronica, stop—
Or what? You'll **spill your lunch** all over me?
You don't have to be **so mean!**
Oh, Betty— defending the crybaby?
Is it because **you're** a crybaby? That's right, I've seen you sniveling down the halls. Upset because Valerie's upgraded to a **new best friend.**
So tragic.

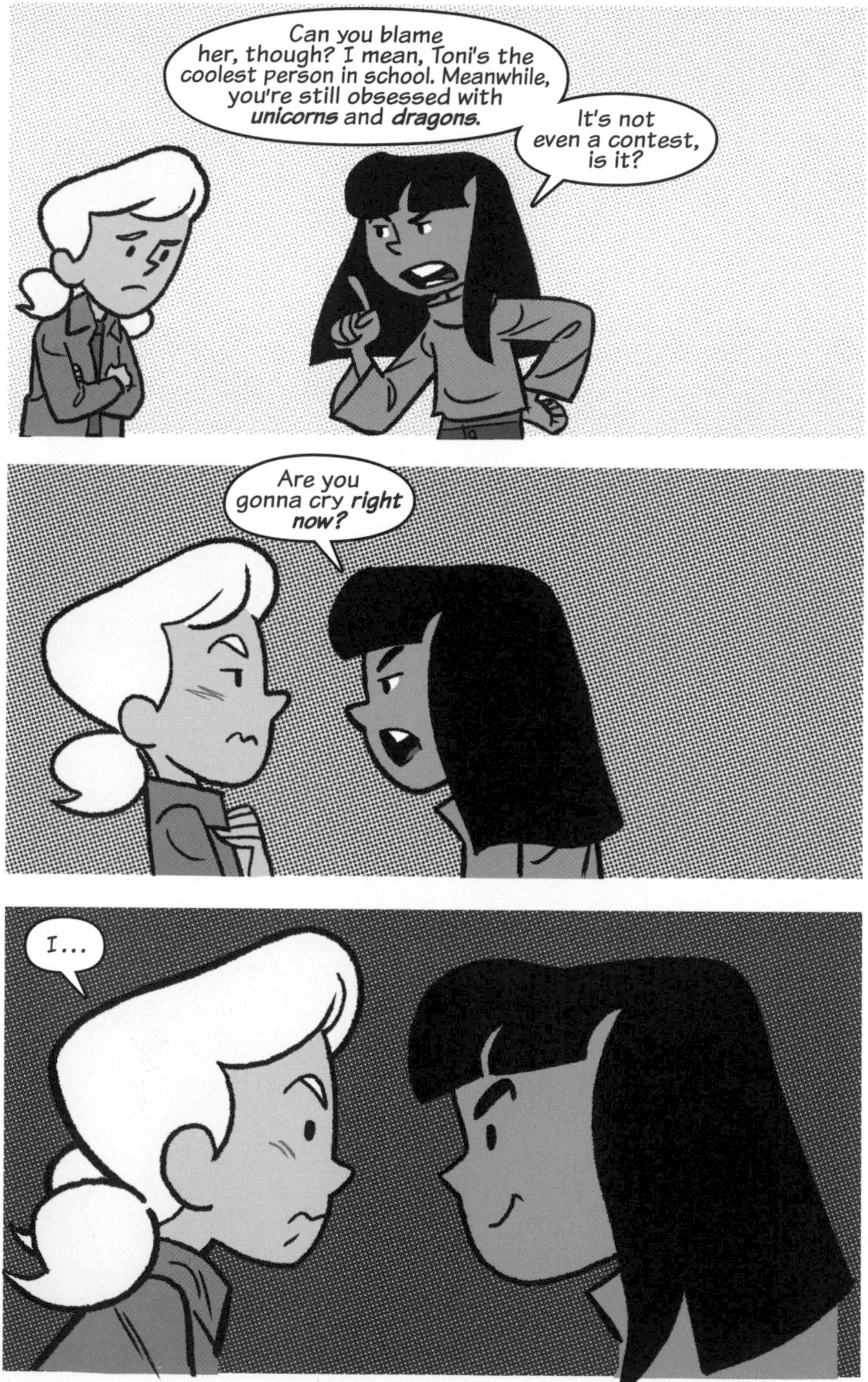
Can you blame her, though? I mean, Toni's the coolest person in school. Meanwhile, you're still obsessed with ***unicorns*** and ***dragons***.
It's not even a contest, is it?
Are you gonna cry ***right now?***
I...

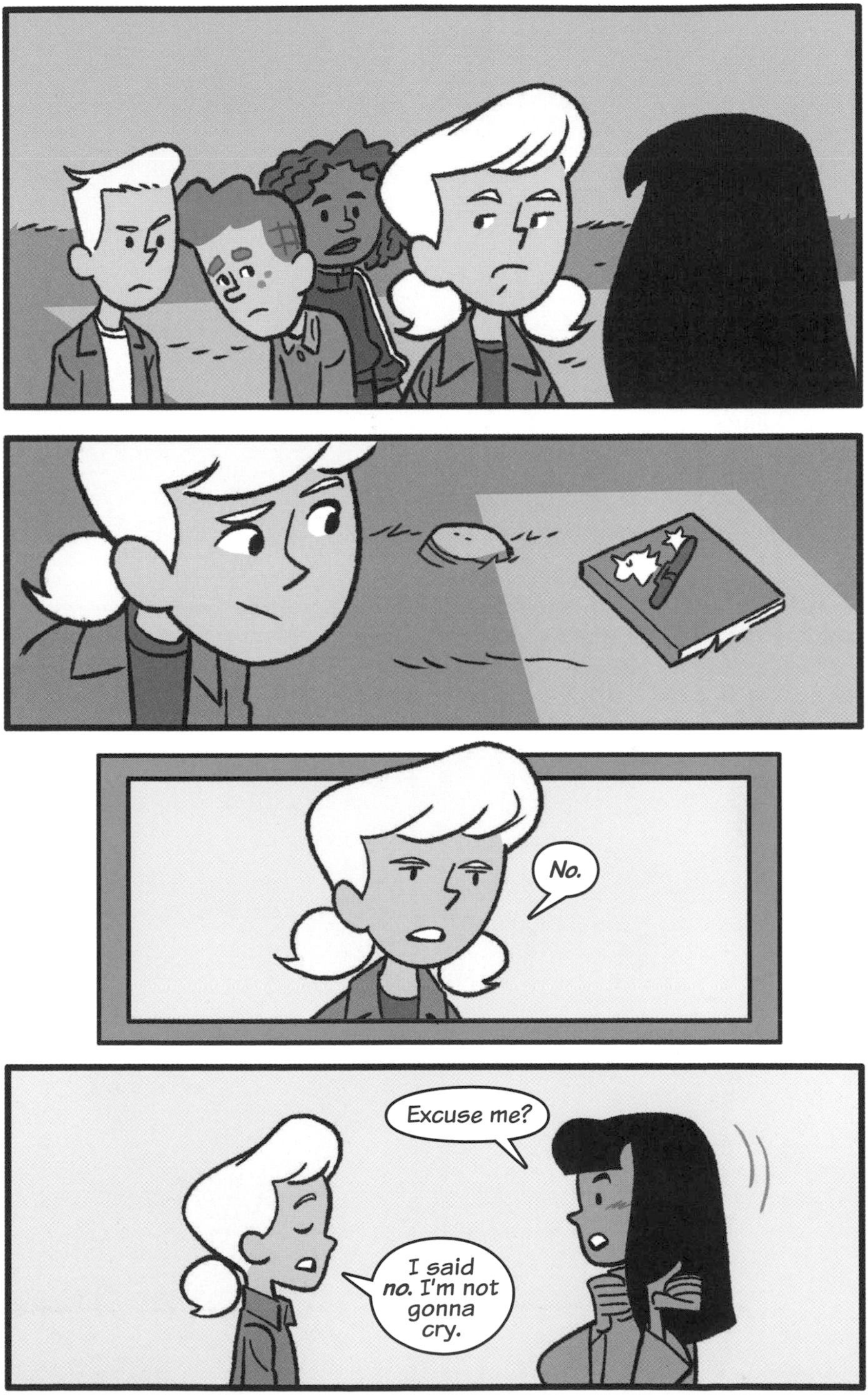
No.
Excuse me?
I said *no.* I'm not gonna cry.

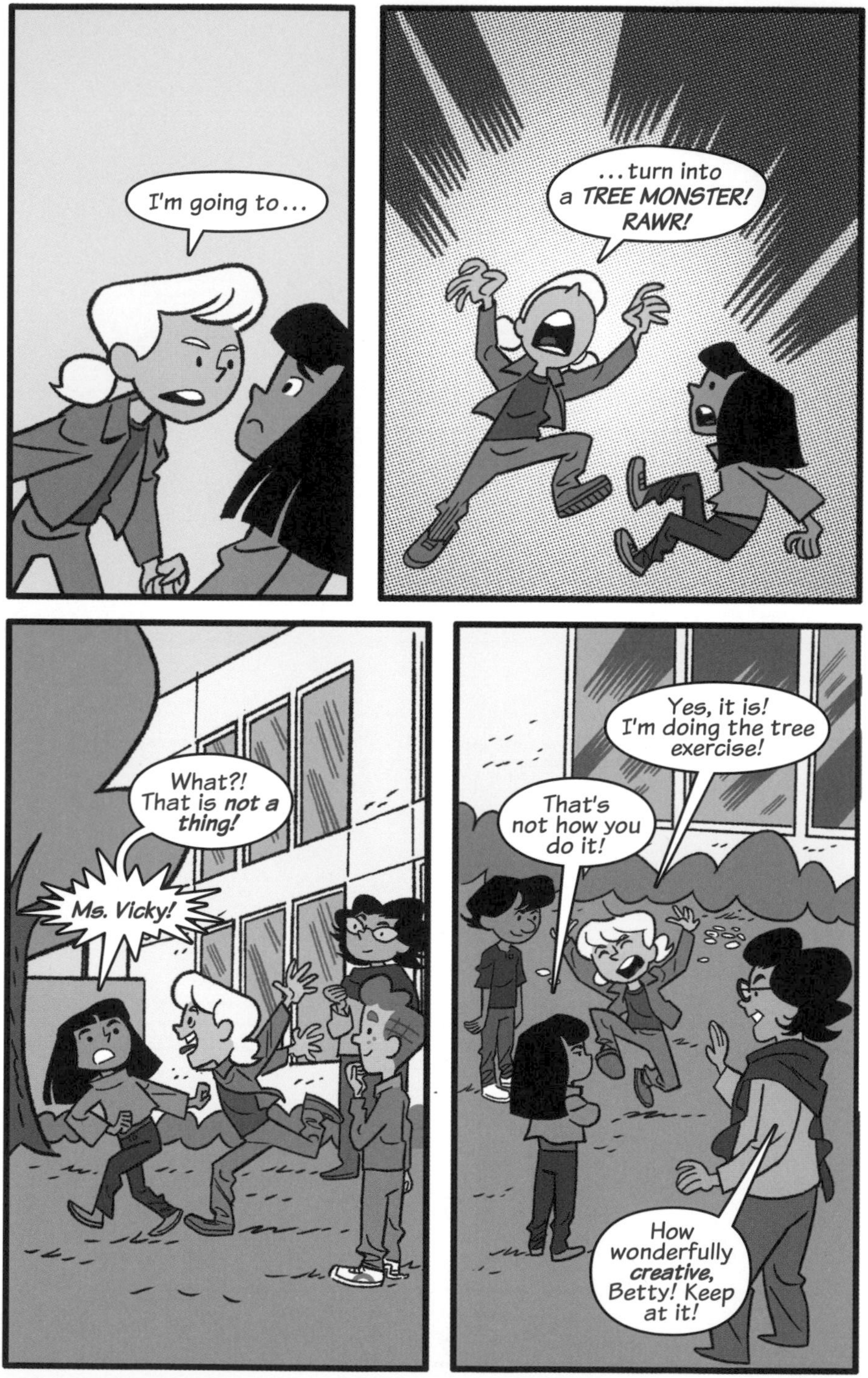
I'm going to...
...turn into a TREE MONSTER! RAWR!
Ms. Vicky!
What?! That is not a thing!
Yes, it is! I'm doing the tree exercise!
That's not how you do it!
How wonderfully creative, Betty! Keep at it!

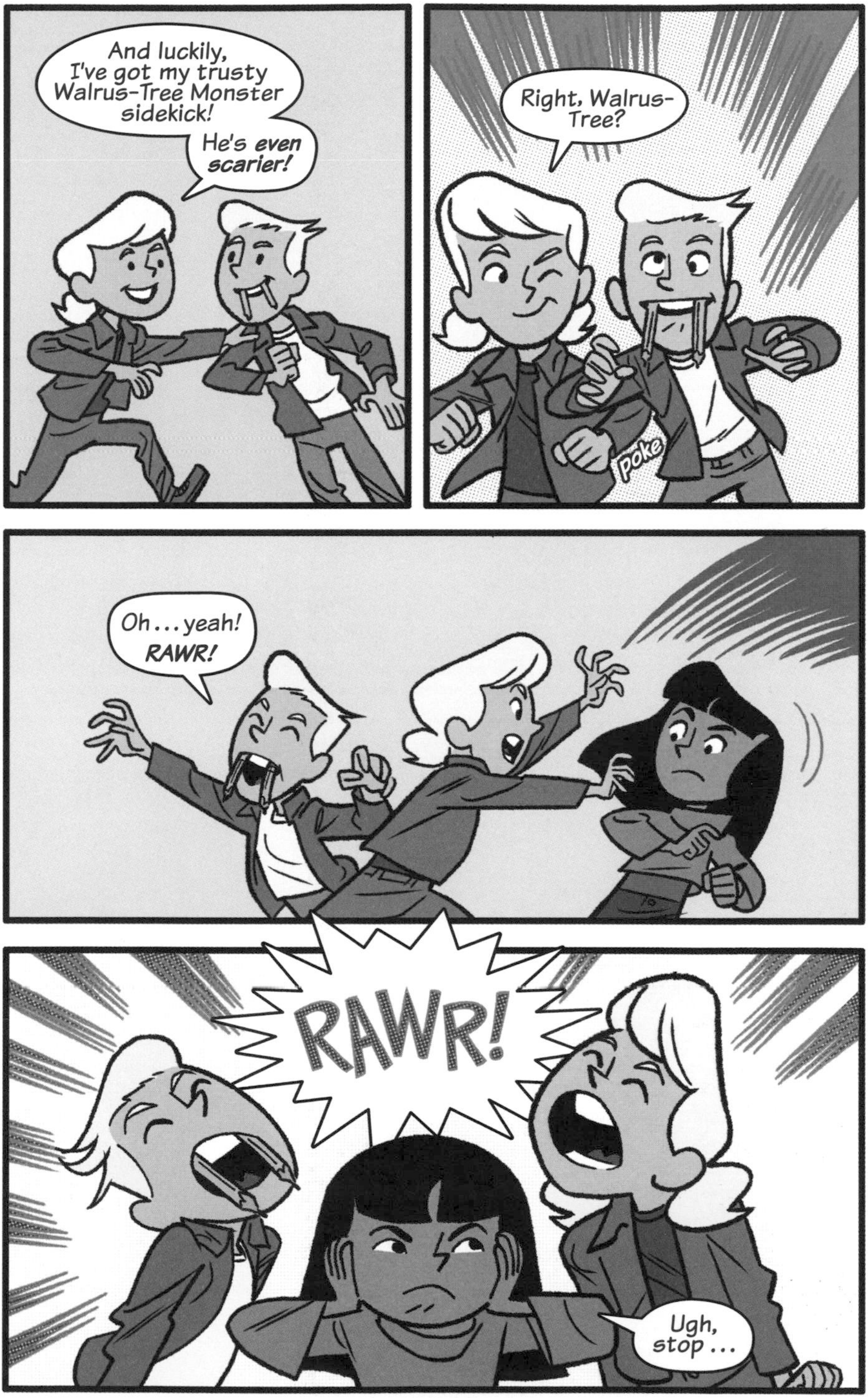
And luckily, I've got my trusty Walrus-Tree Monster sidekick!
He's *even scarier!*
Right, Walrus-Tree?
poke
Oh . . . yeah! **RAWR!**
RAWR!
Ugh, stop . . .

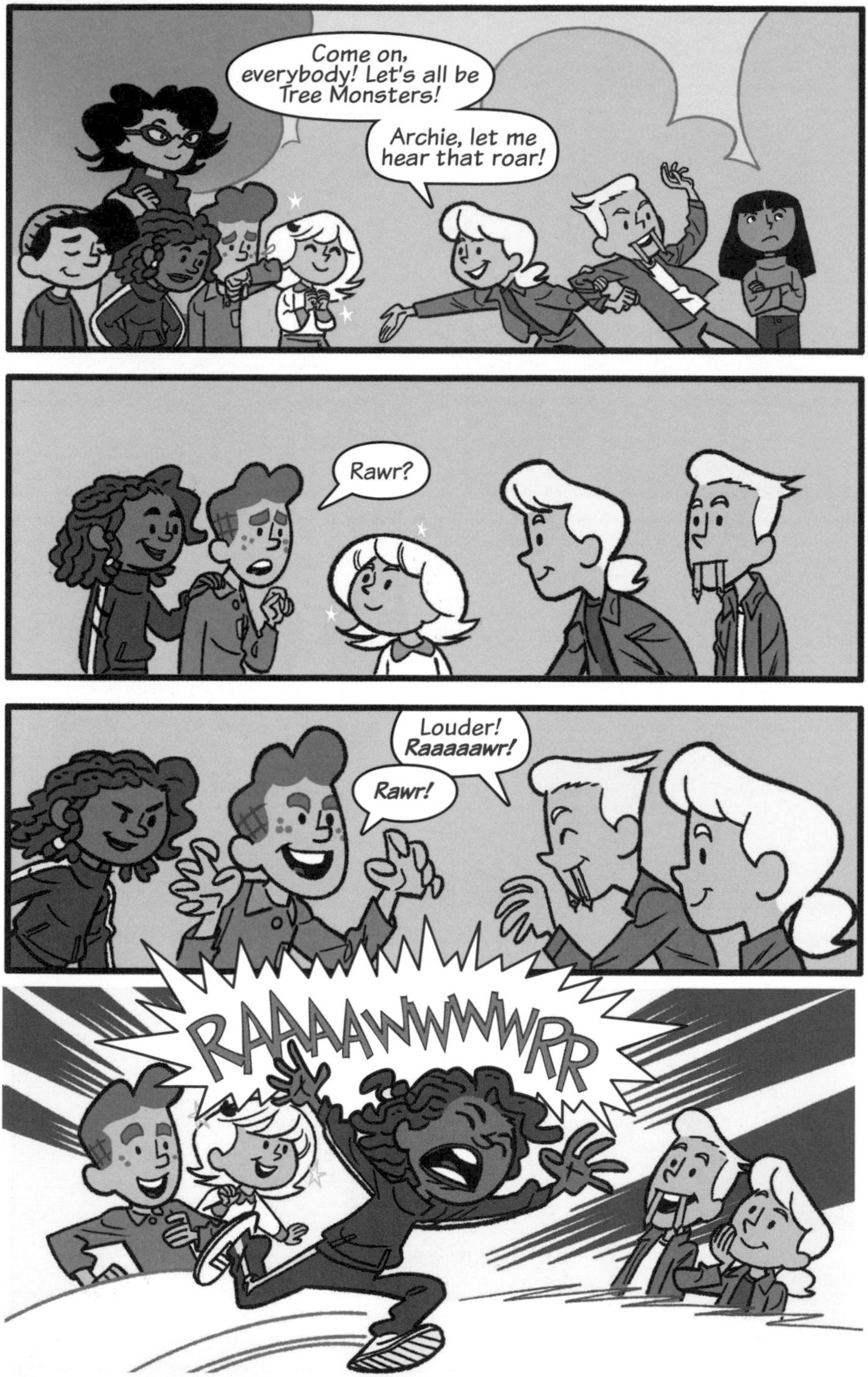
Come on, everybody! Let's all be Tree Monsters!
Archie, let me hear that roar!
Rawr?
Louder! *Raaaaawr!*
Rawr!
RAAAWWWWRR

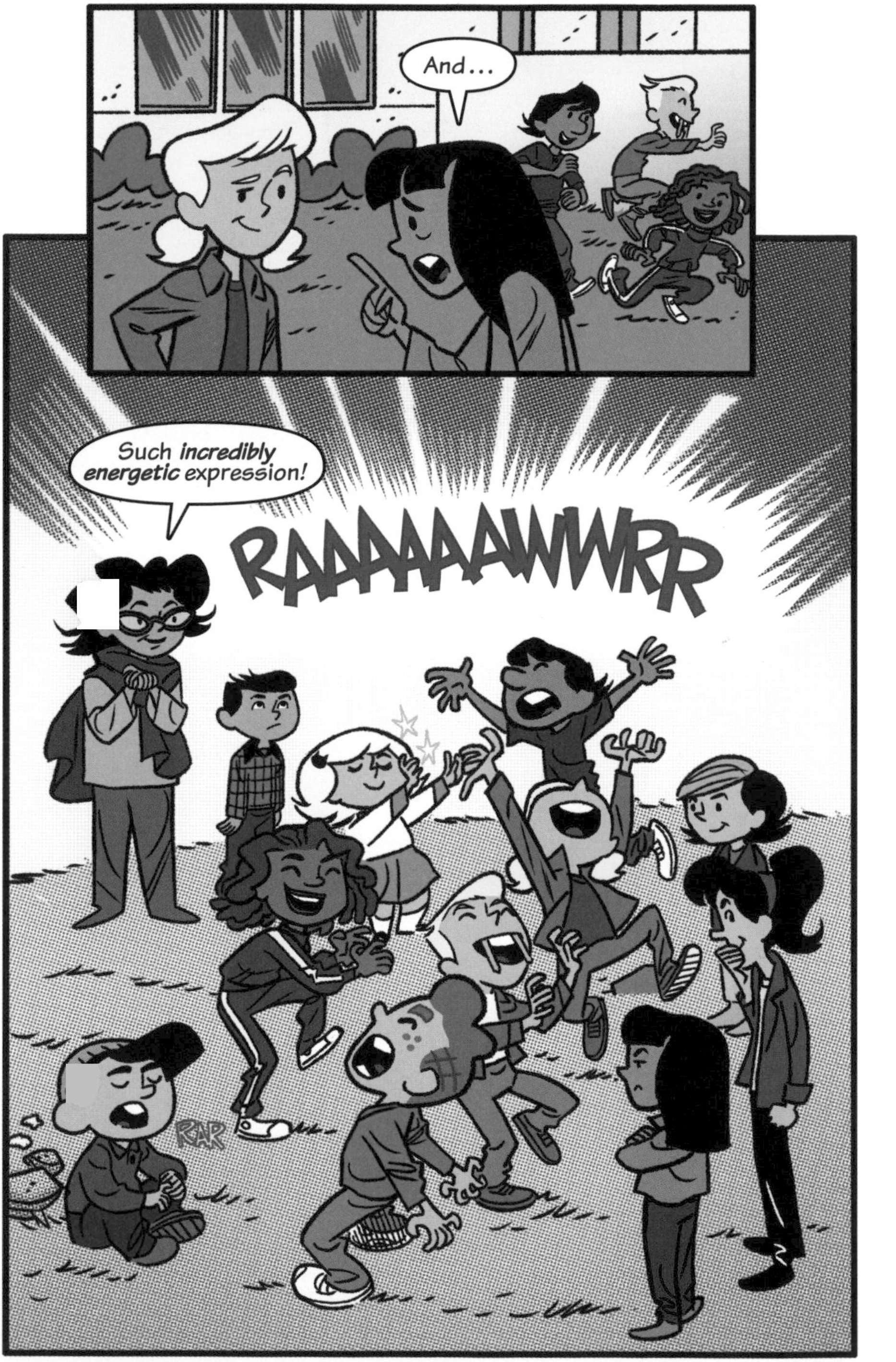
And...
Such *incredibly energetic* expression!
RAAAAAAWWRR
RAR

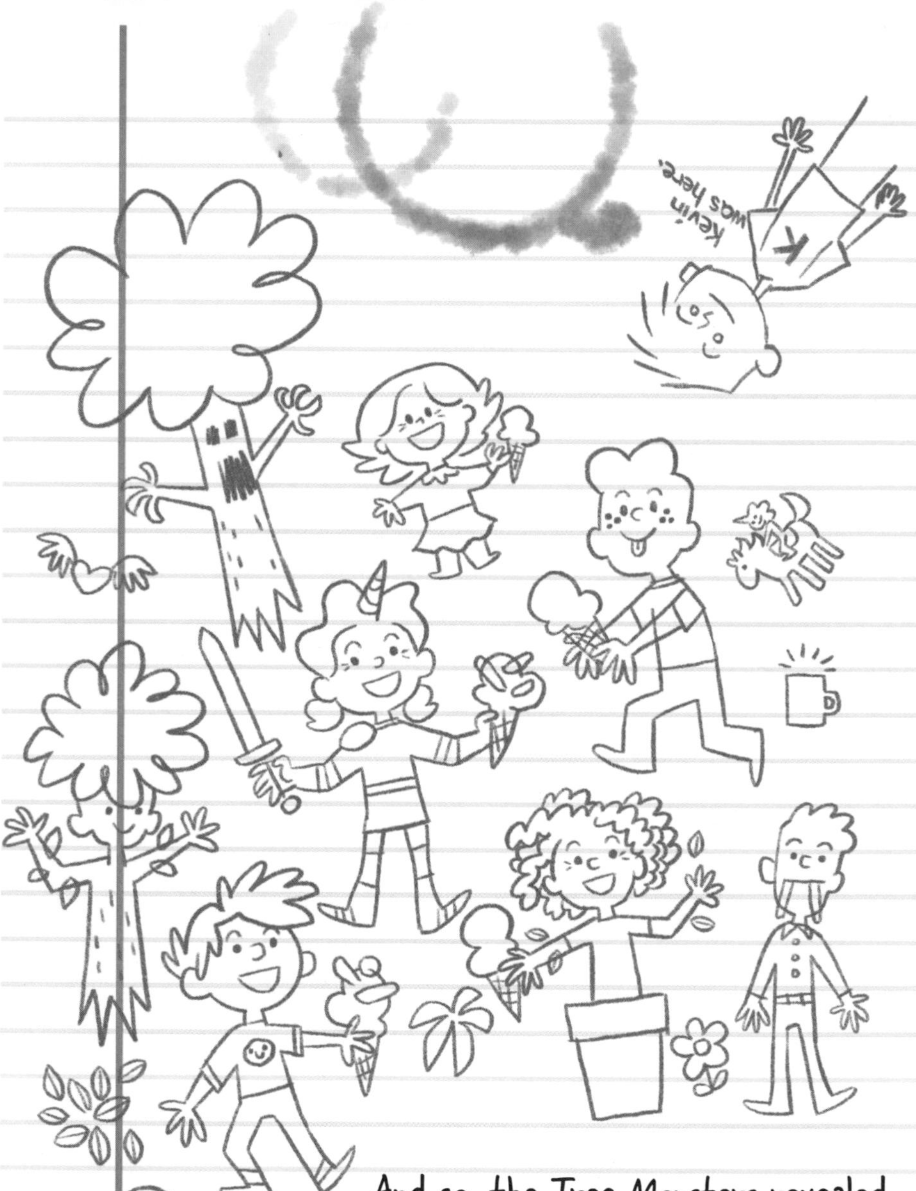
Kevin was here.

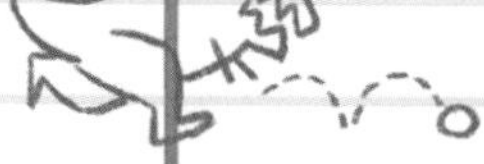

And so, the Tree Monsters revealed themselves to be friends rather than foes—they were not a mighty evil for the knights to defeat, but a force for good. And they made truly excellent ice cream.

70

71

72

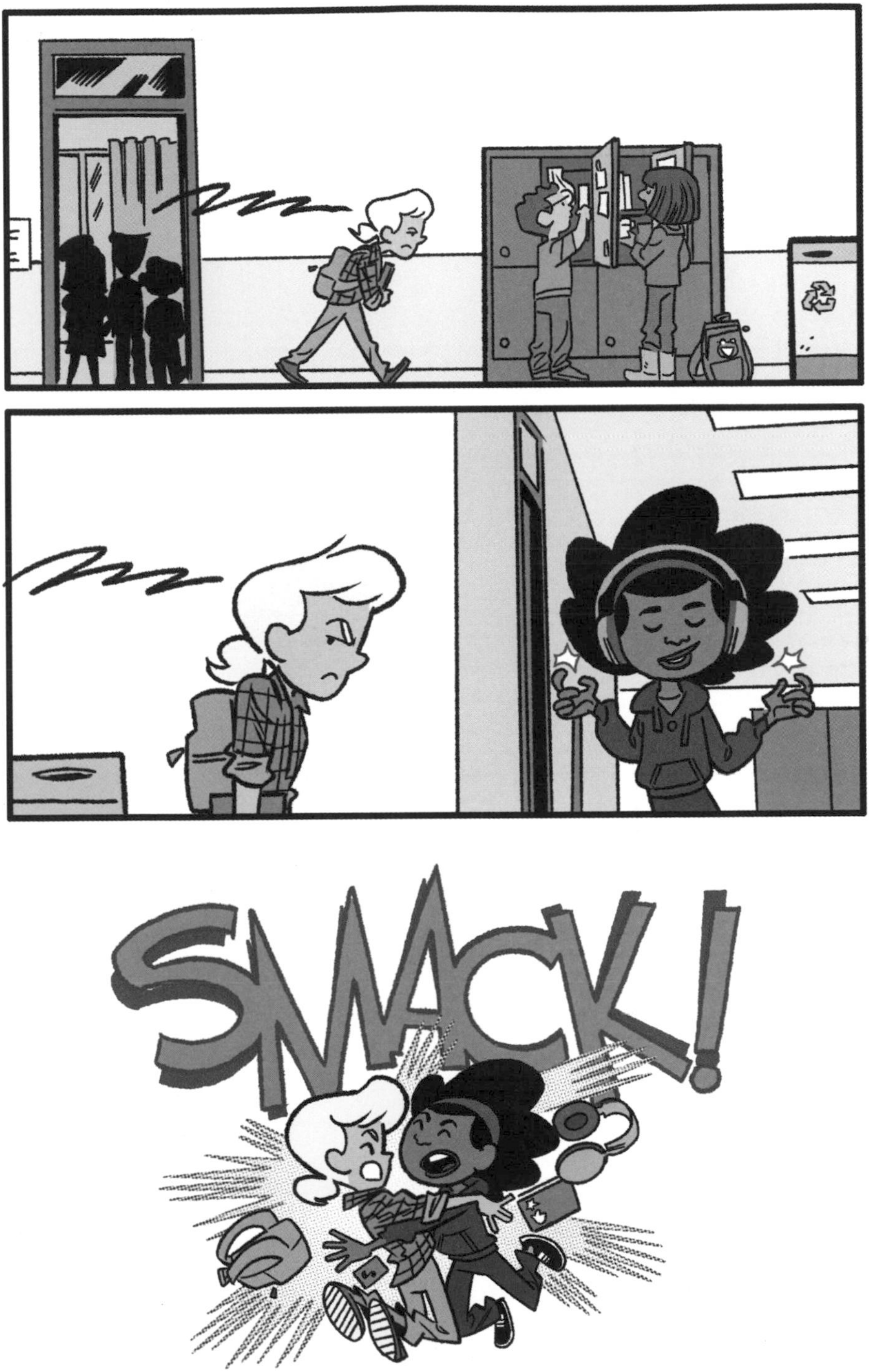
SMACK!

74

75

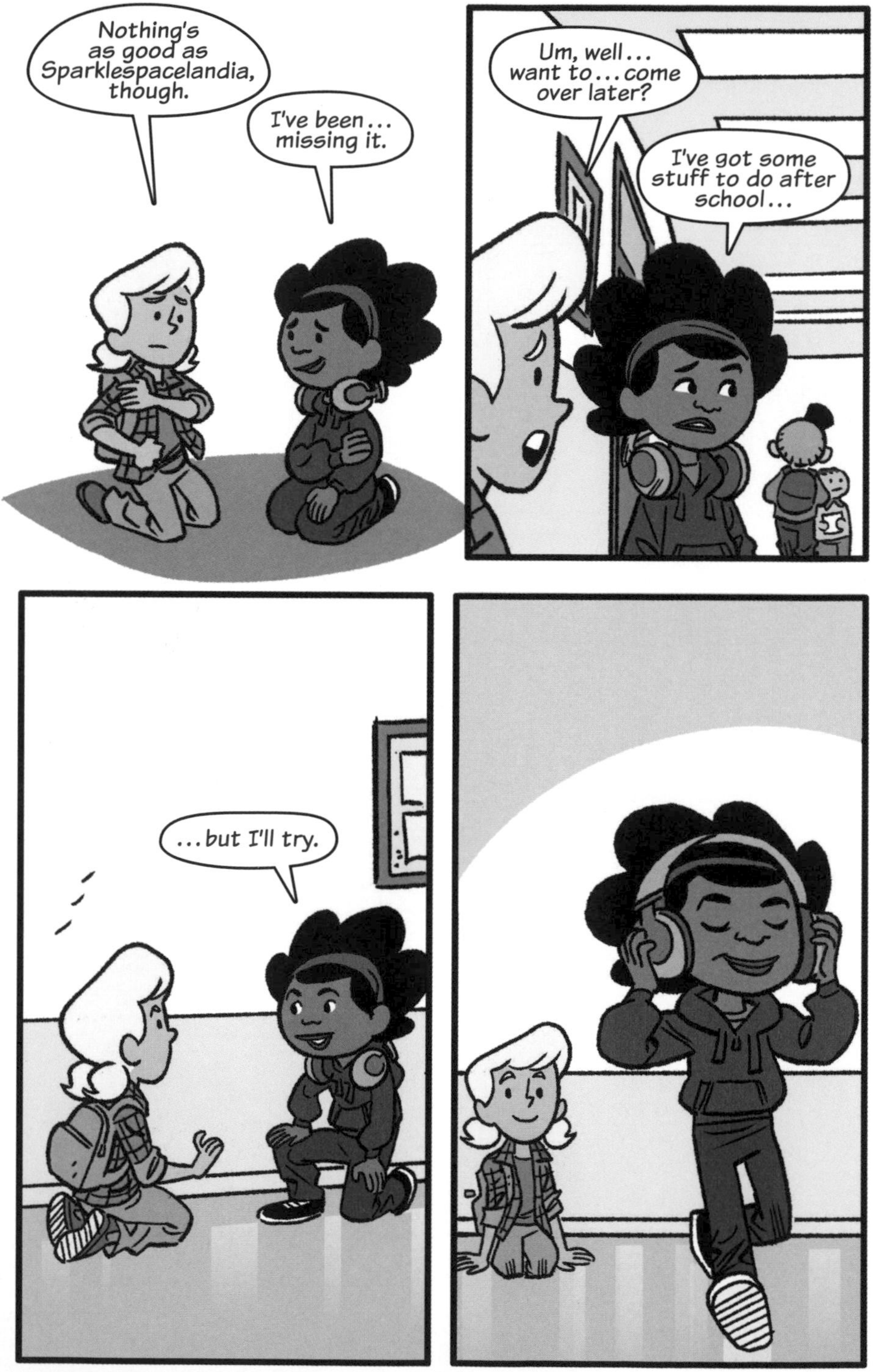
Nothing's as good as Sparklespacelandia, though.
I've been... missing it.
Um, well... want to... come over later?
I've got some stuff to do after school...
...but I'll try.

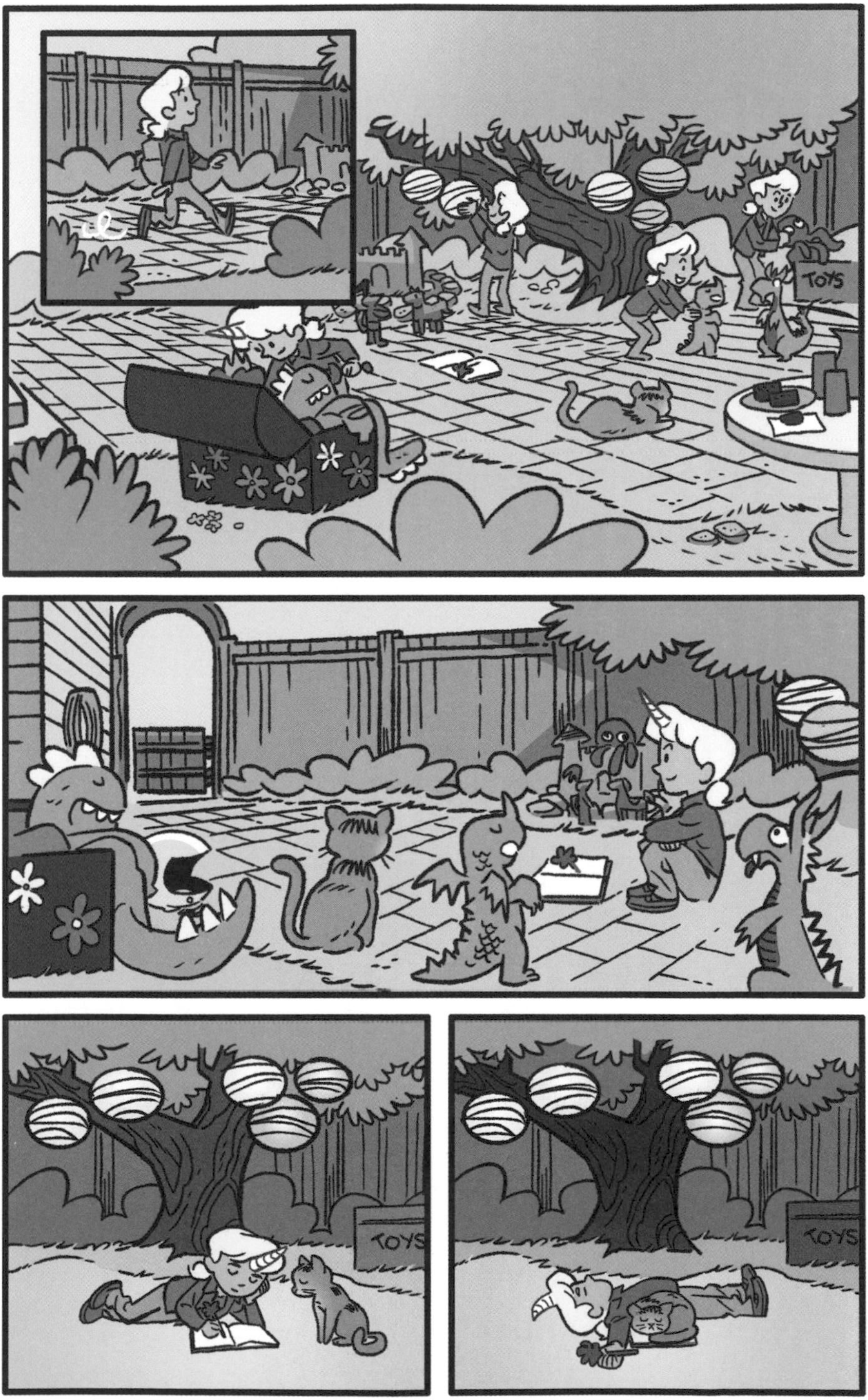
TOYS
TOYS
TOYS

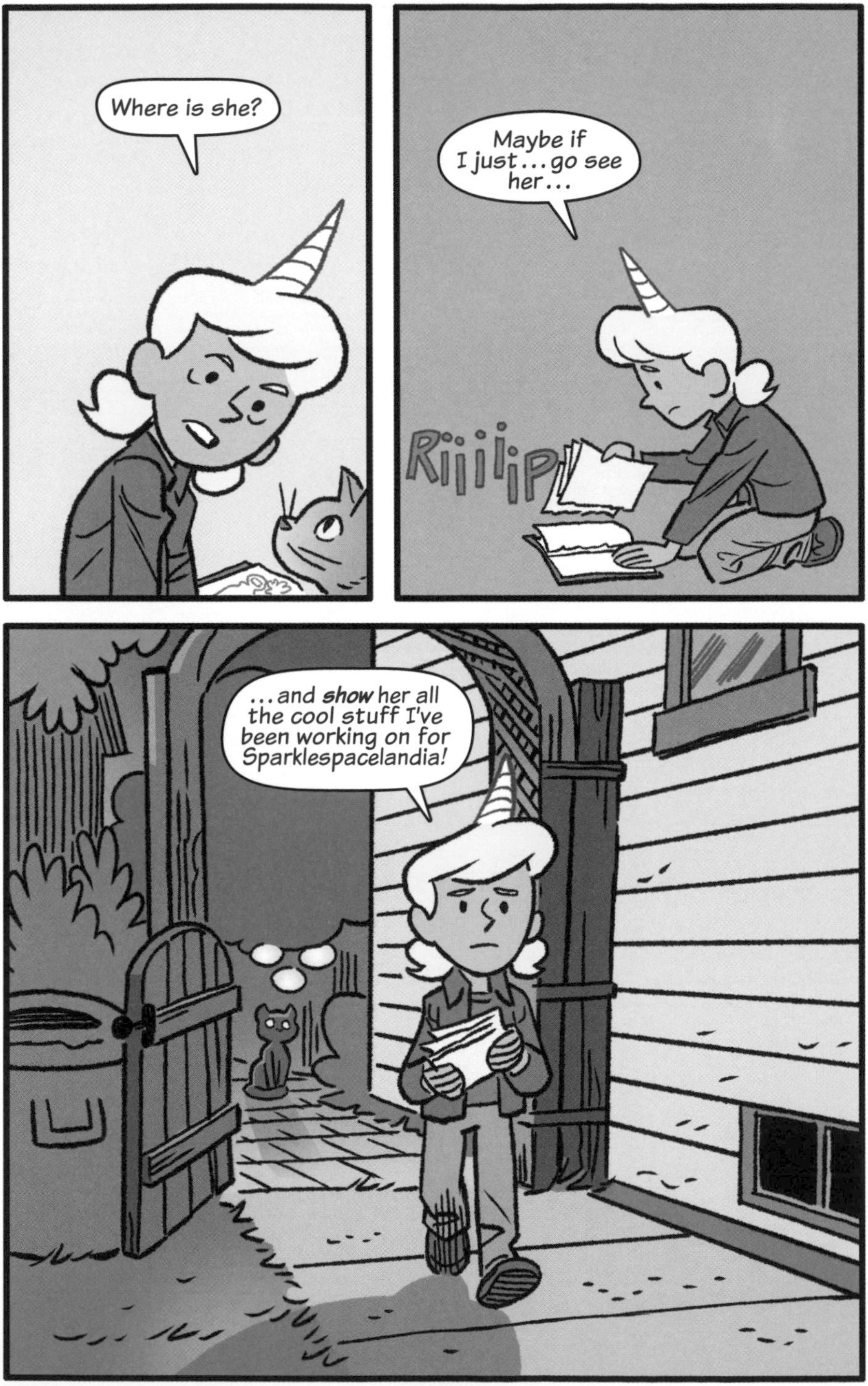
Where is she?
Maybe if I just... go see her...
RIIIIIP
...and show her all the cool stuff I've been working on for Sparklespacelandia!

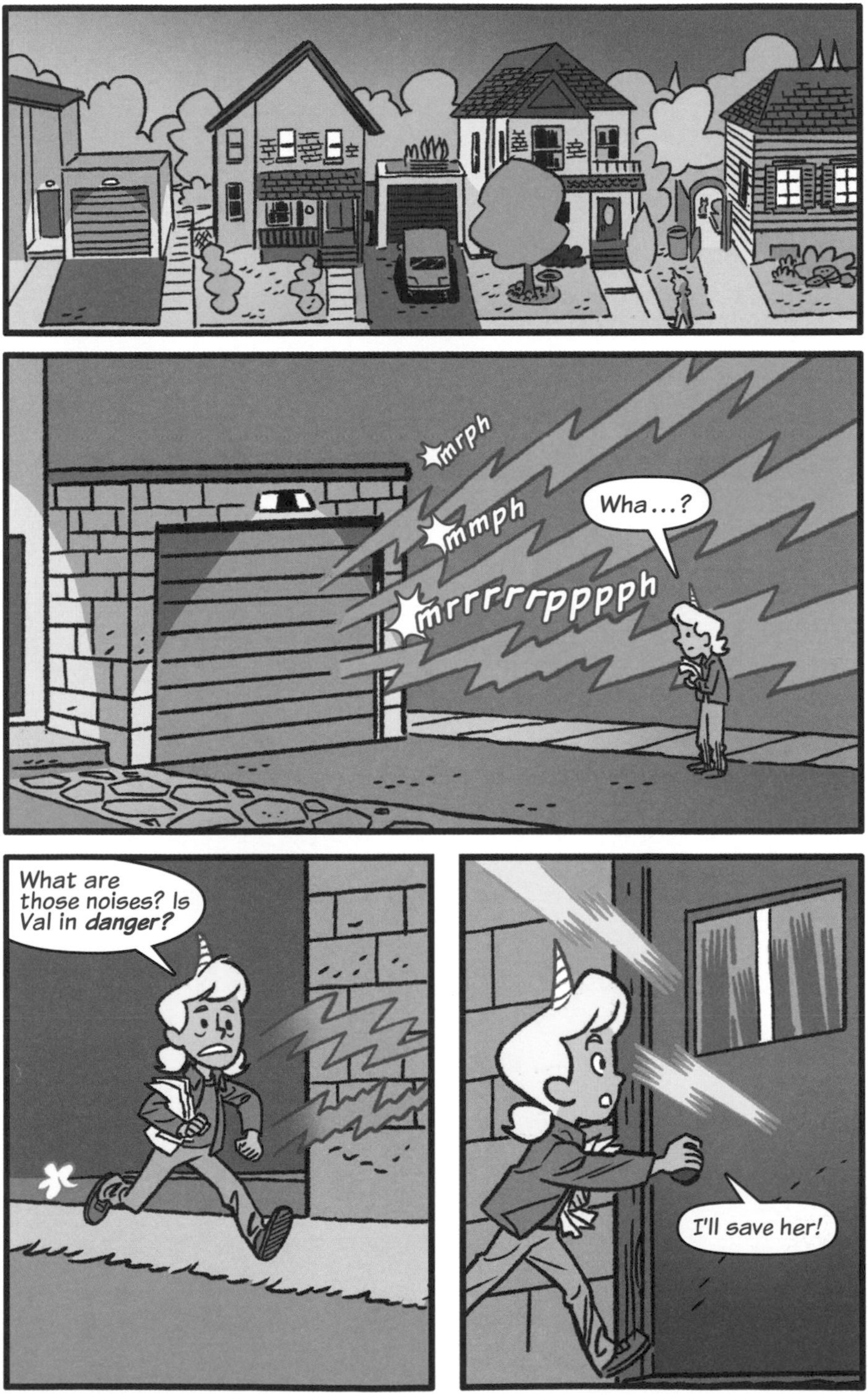
mrph
mmph
mrrrrrpppph
Wha...?
What are those noises? Is Val in *danger?*
I'll save her!

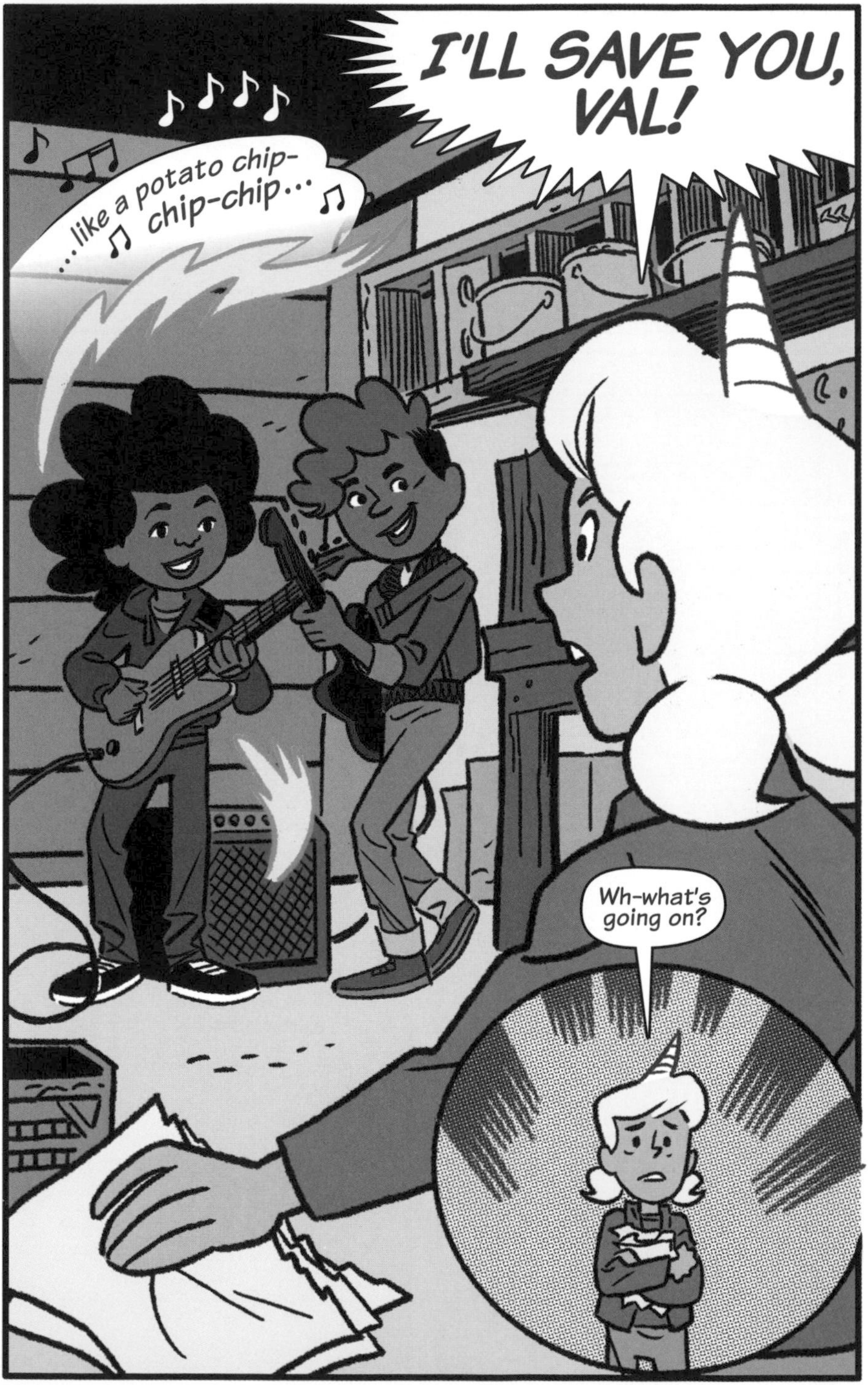
...like a potato chip-chip-chip...
I'LL SAVE YOU, VAL!
Wh-what's going on?

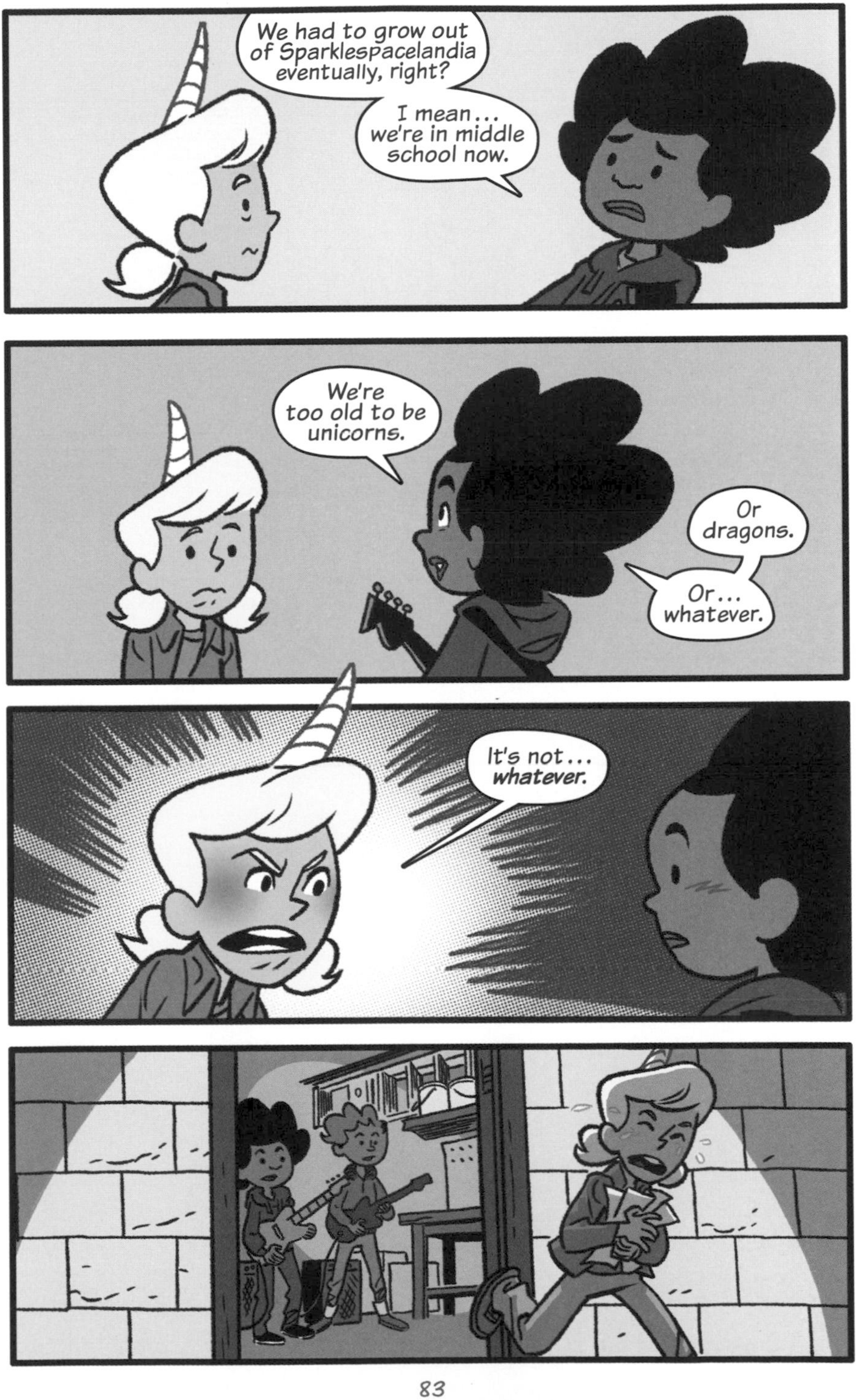
We had to grow out of Sparklespacelandia eventually, right?
I mean... we're in middle school now.
We're too old to be unicorns.
Or dragons.
Or... whatever.
It's not... *whatever.*

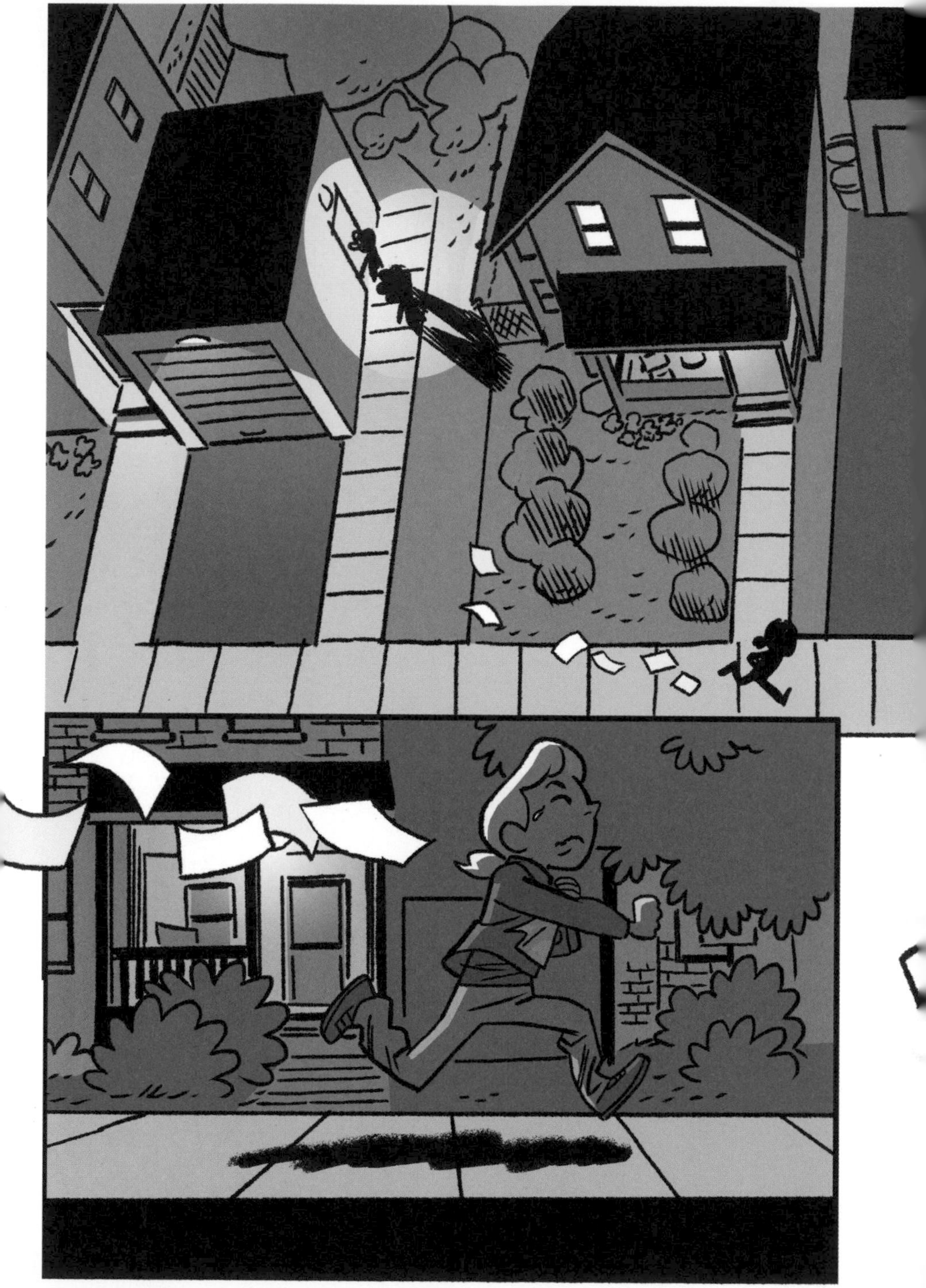

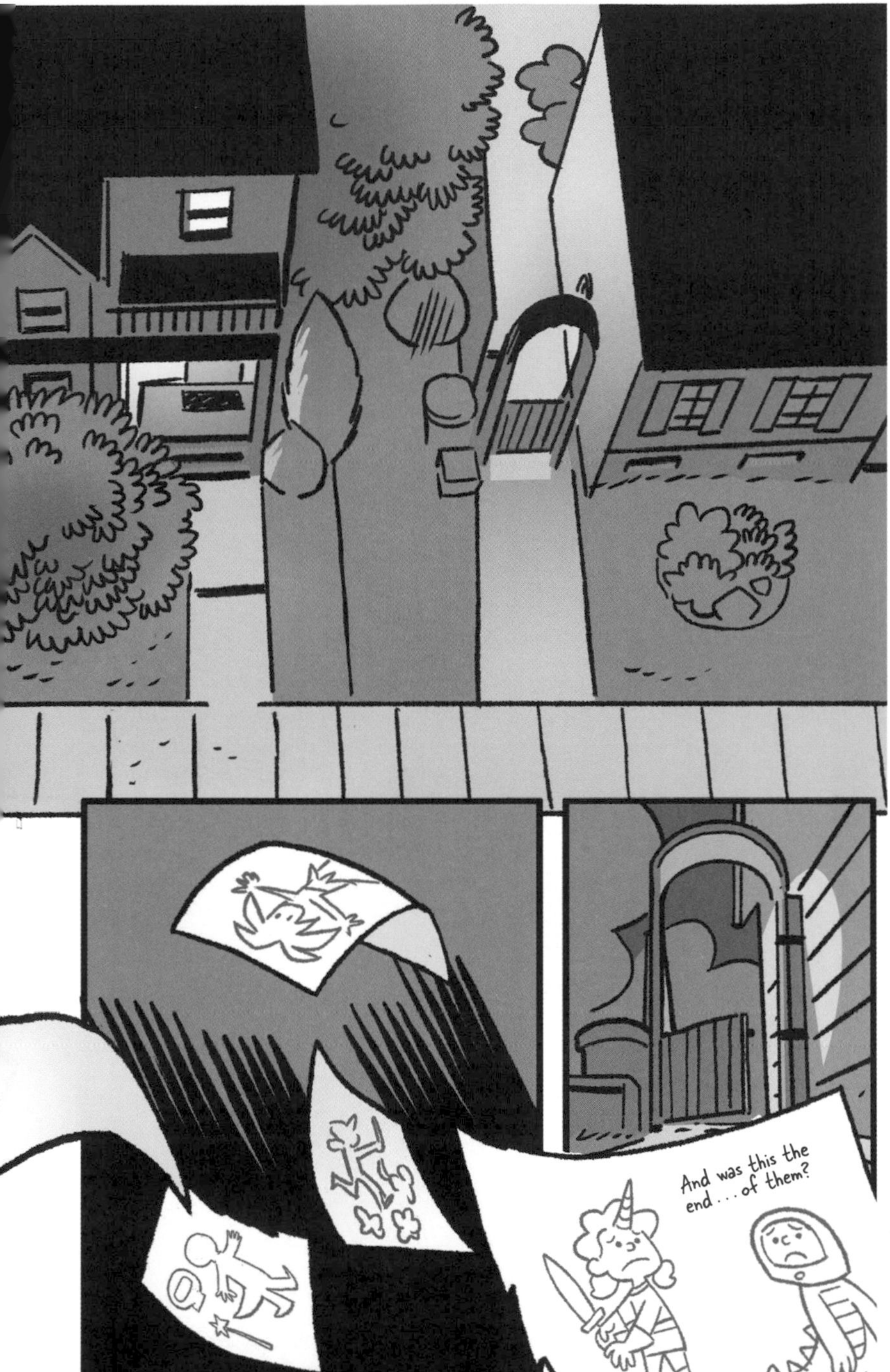
And was this the end . . . of them?

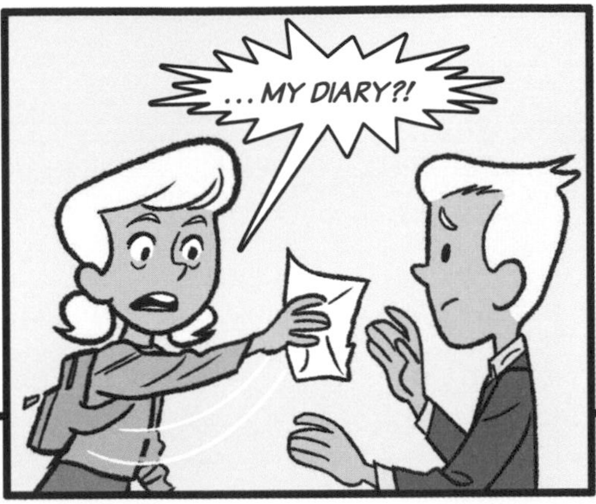
...MY DIARY?!

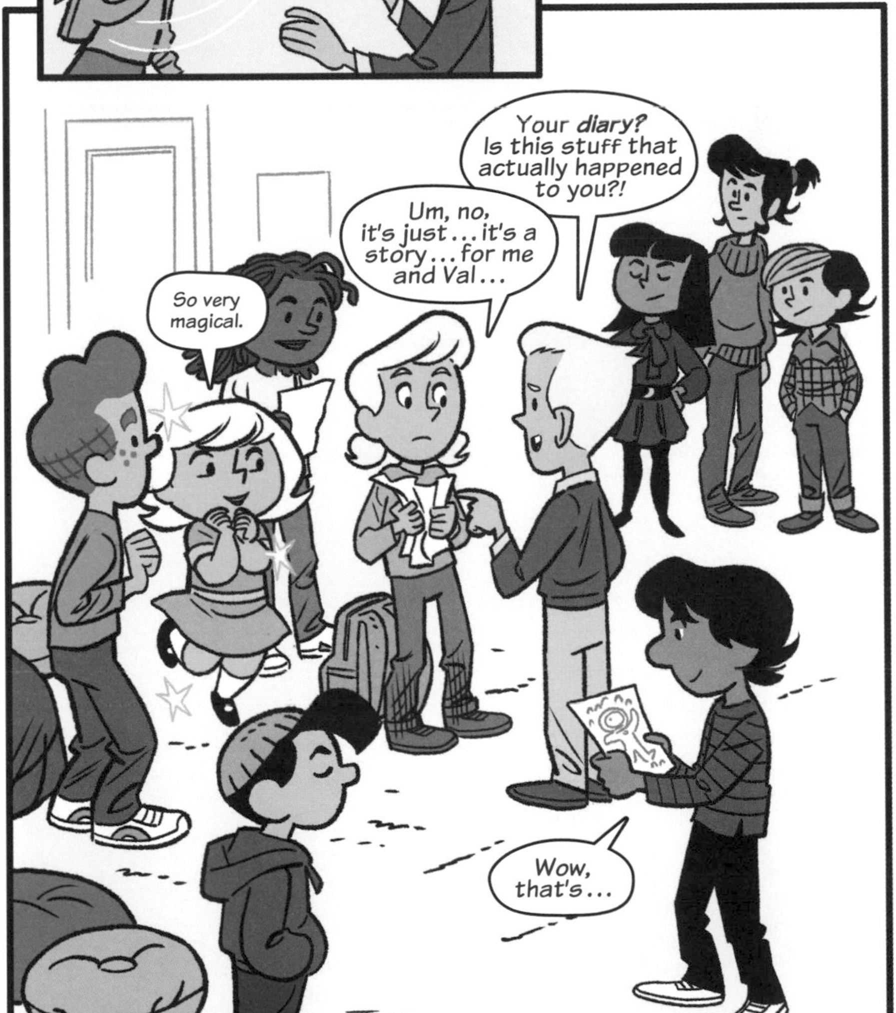
So very magical.
Um, no, it's just... it's a story... for me and Val...
Your diary? Is this stuff that actually happened to you?!
Wow, that's...

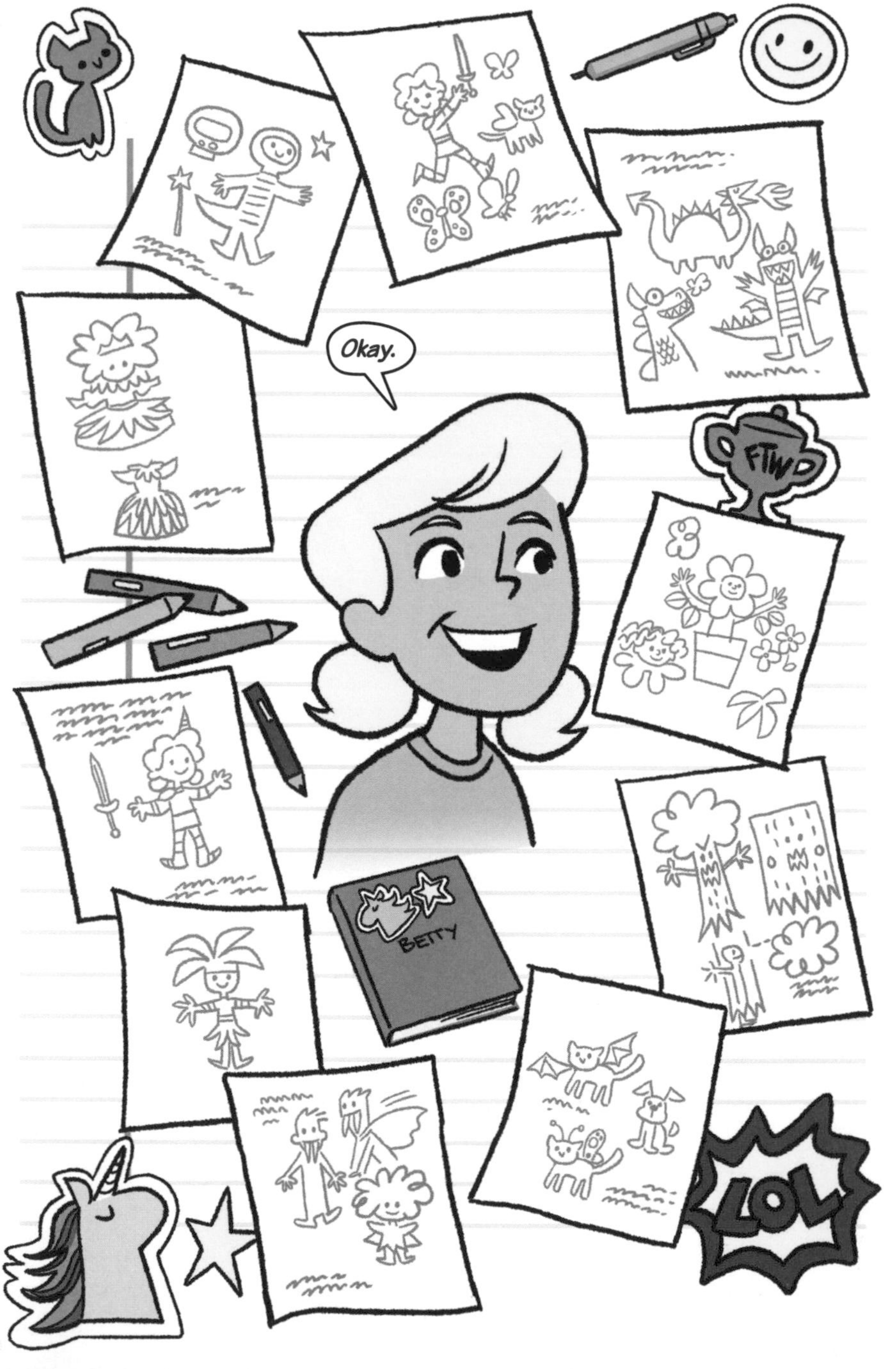
Okay.
FTW
BETTY
LOL

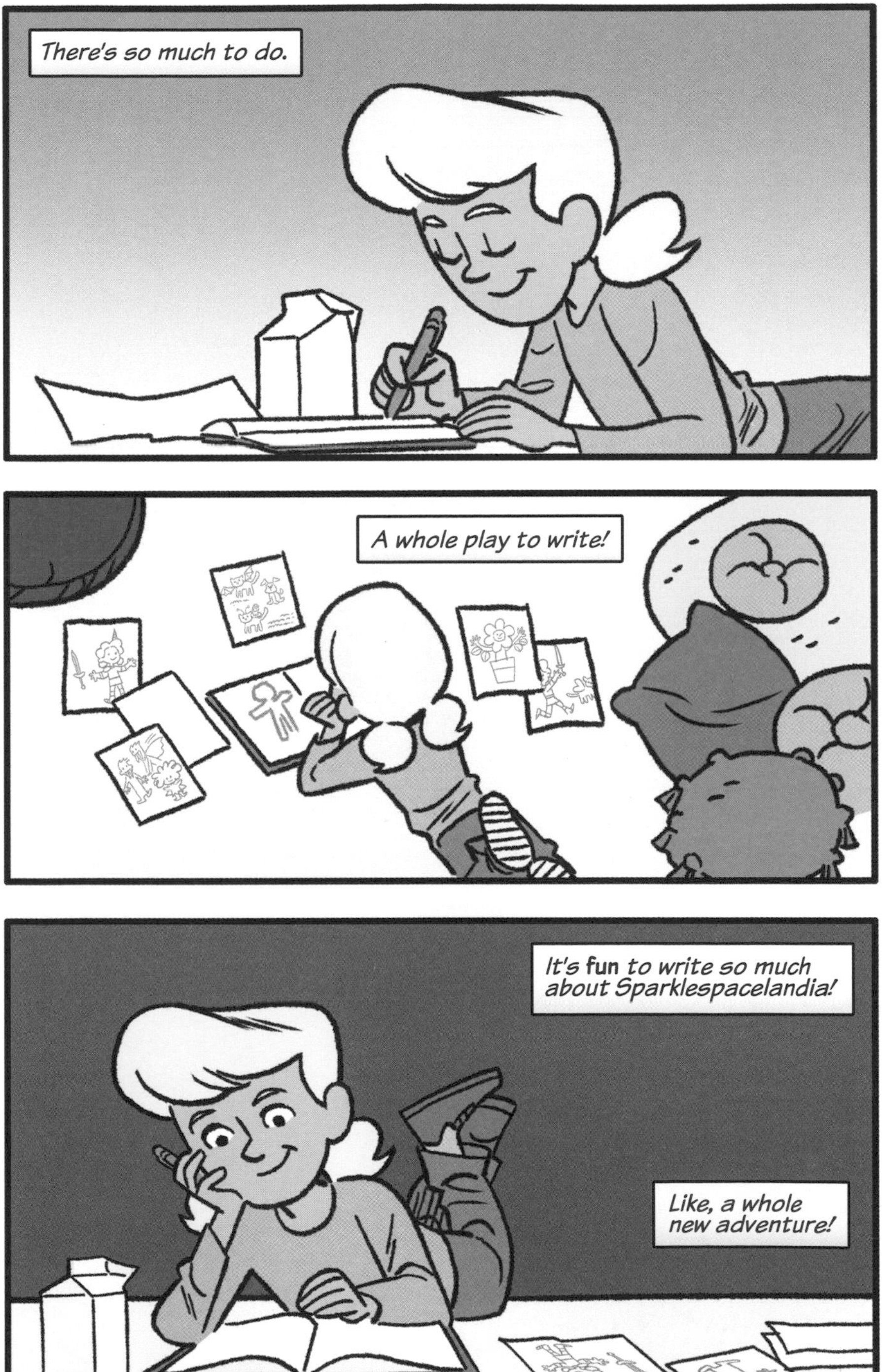
There's so much to do.
A whole play to write!
It's fun to write so much about Sparklespacelandia!
Like, a whole new adventure!

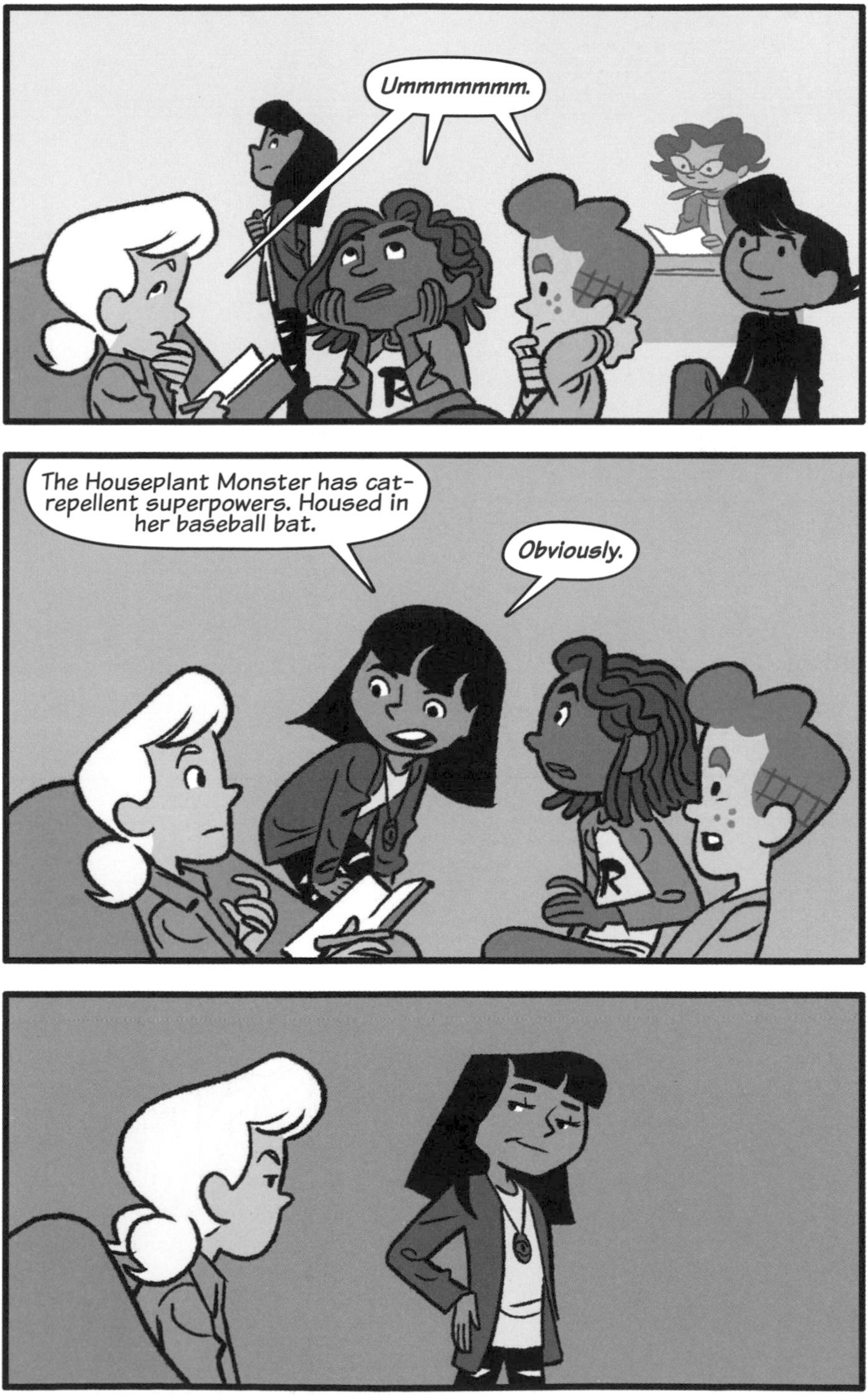
Ummmmmmm.
The Houseplant Monster has cat-repellent superpowers. Housed in her baseball bat.
Obviously.

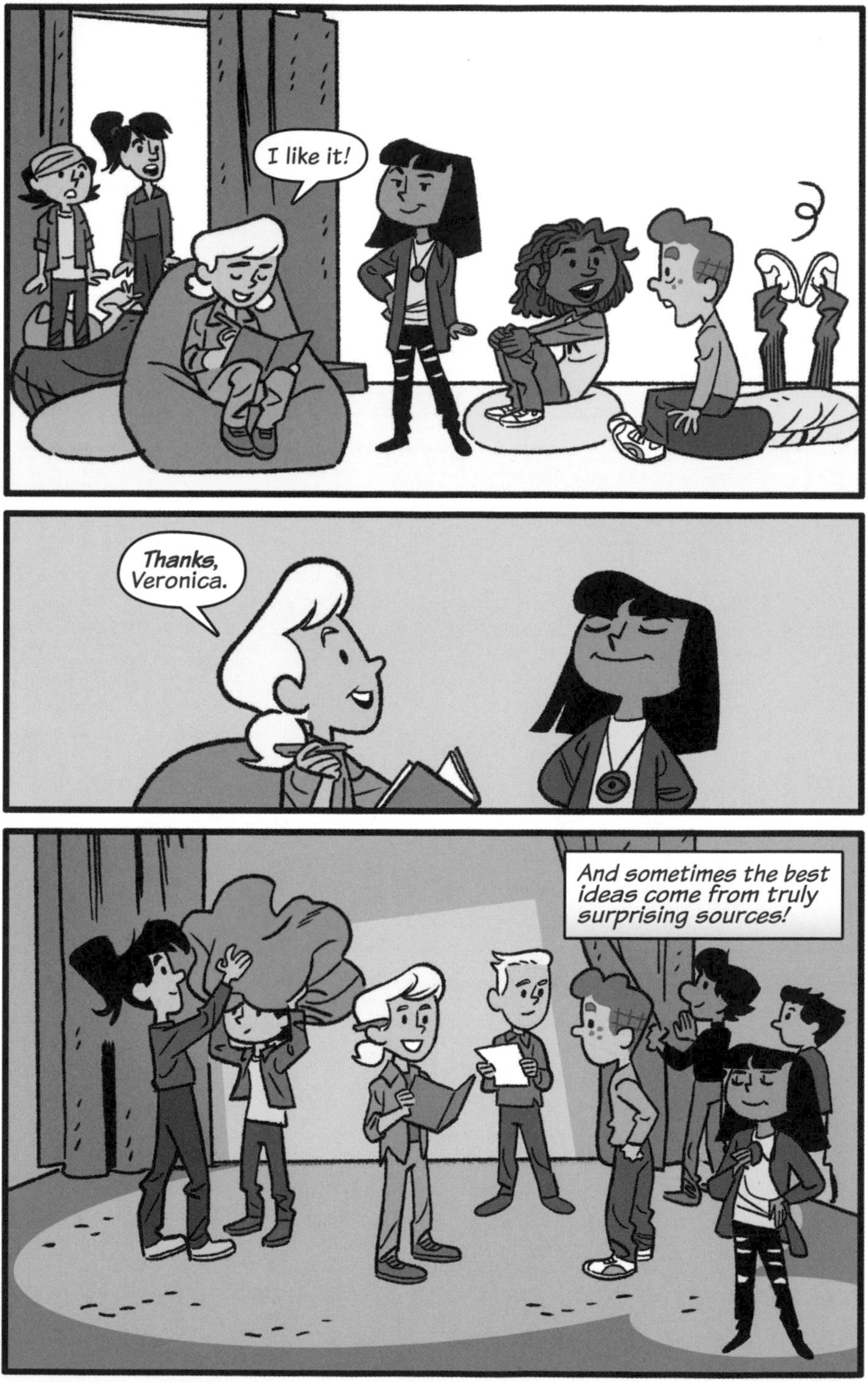
I like it!
Thanks, Veronica.
And sometimes the best ideas come from truly surprising sources!

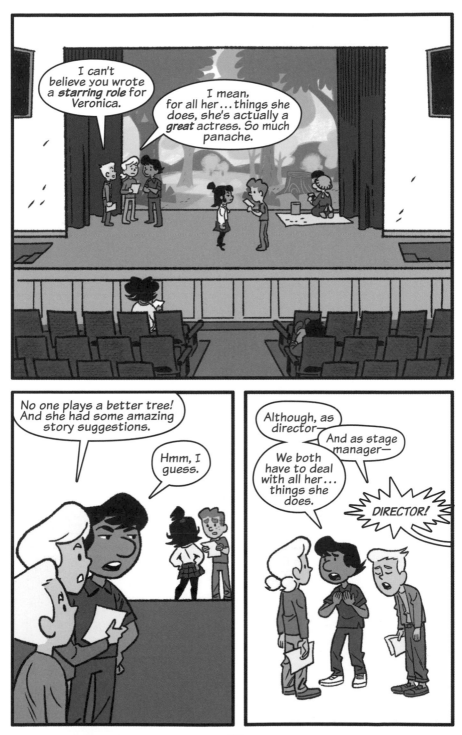

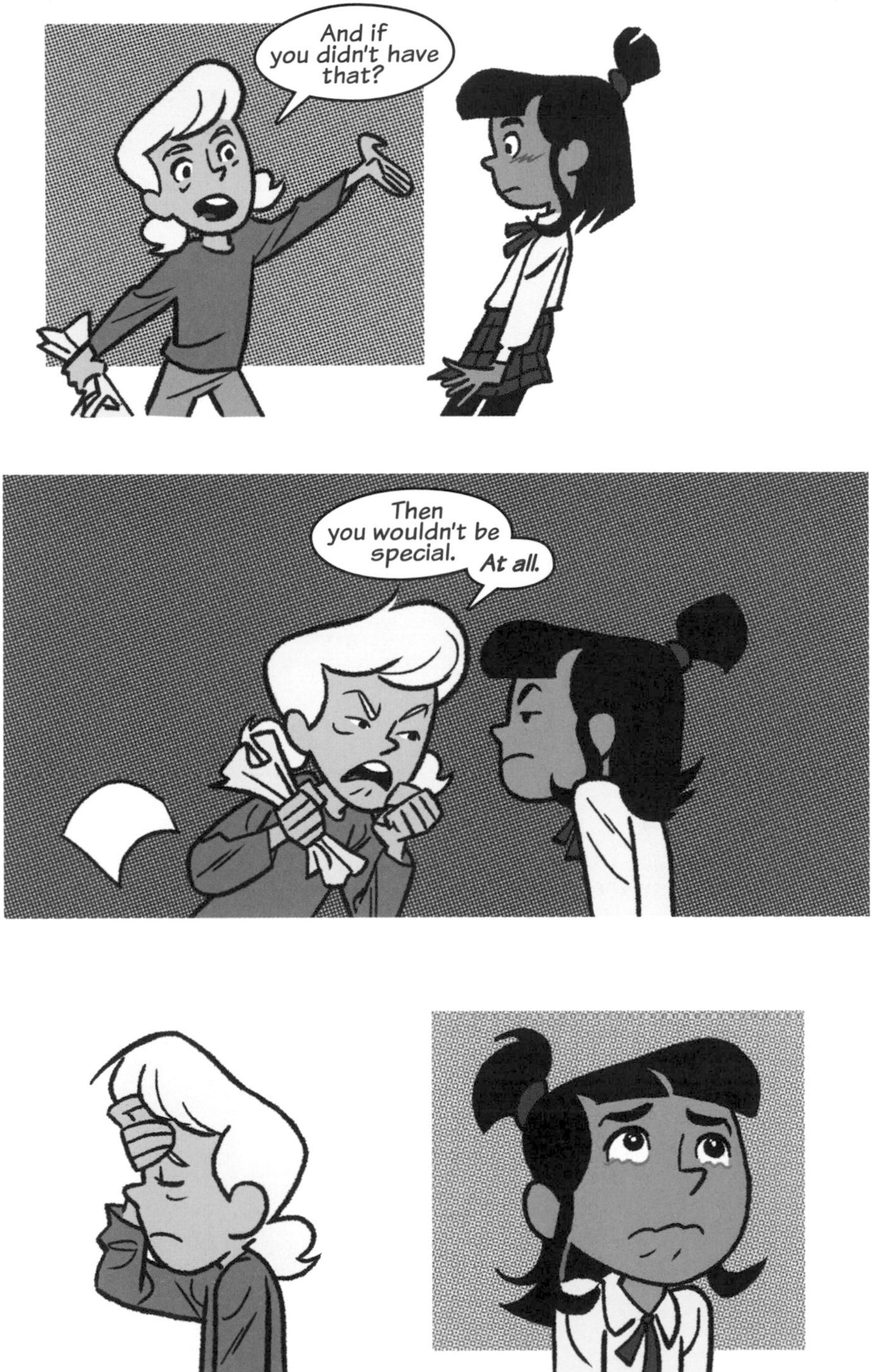

And if you didn't have that?
Then you wouldn't be special.
At all.

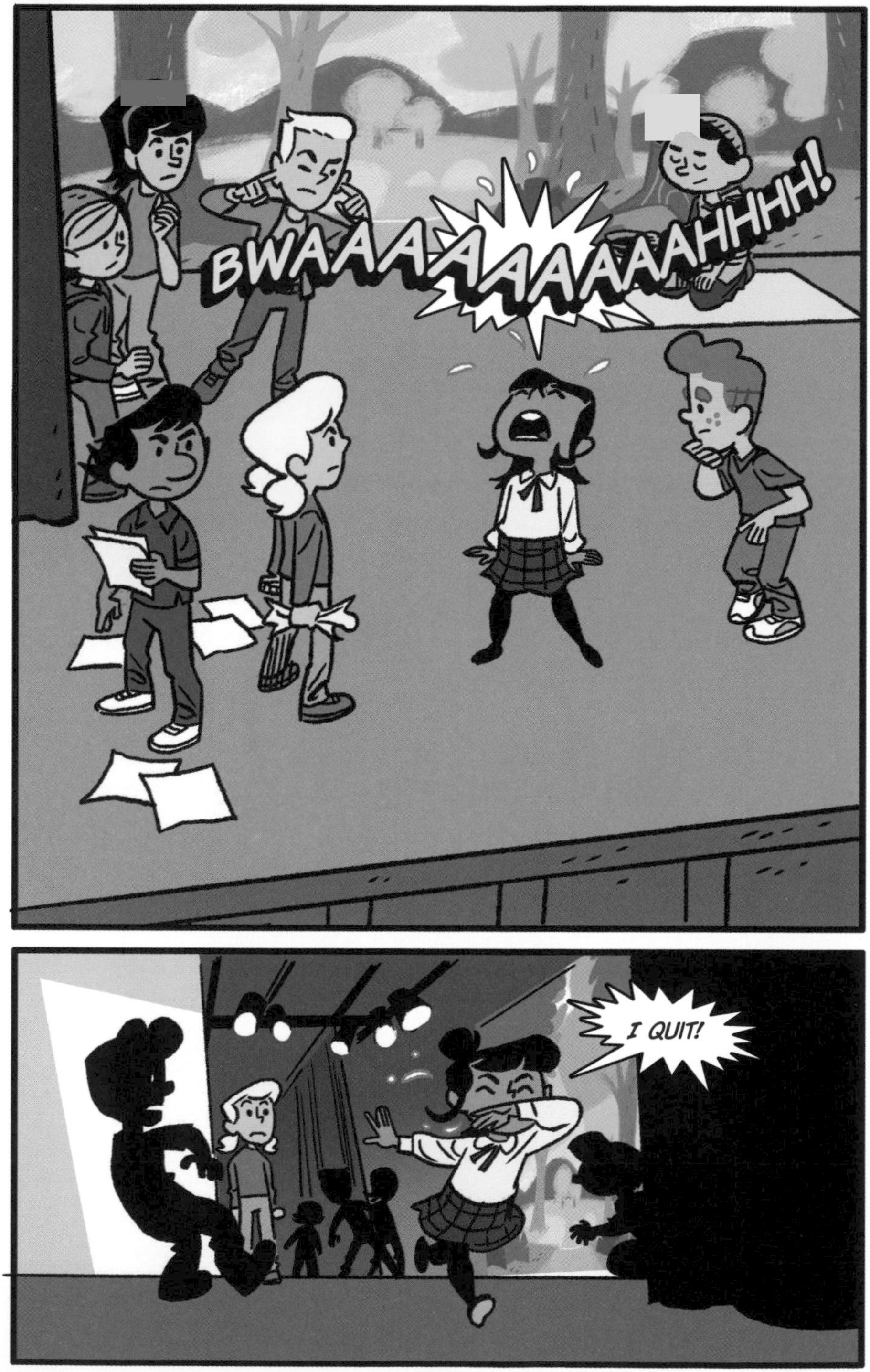
BWAAAAAAAAAHHHH!
I QUIT!

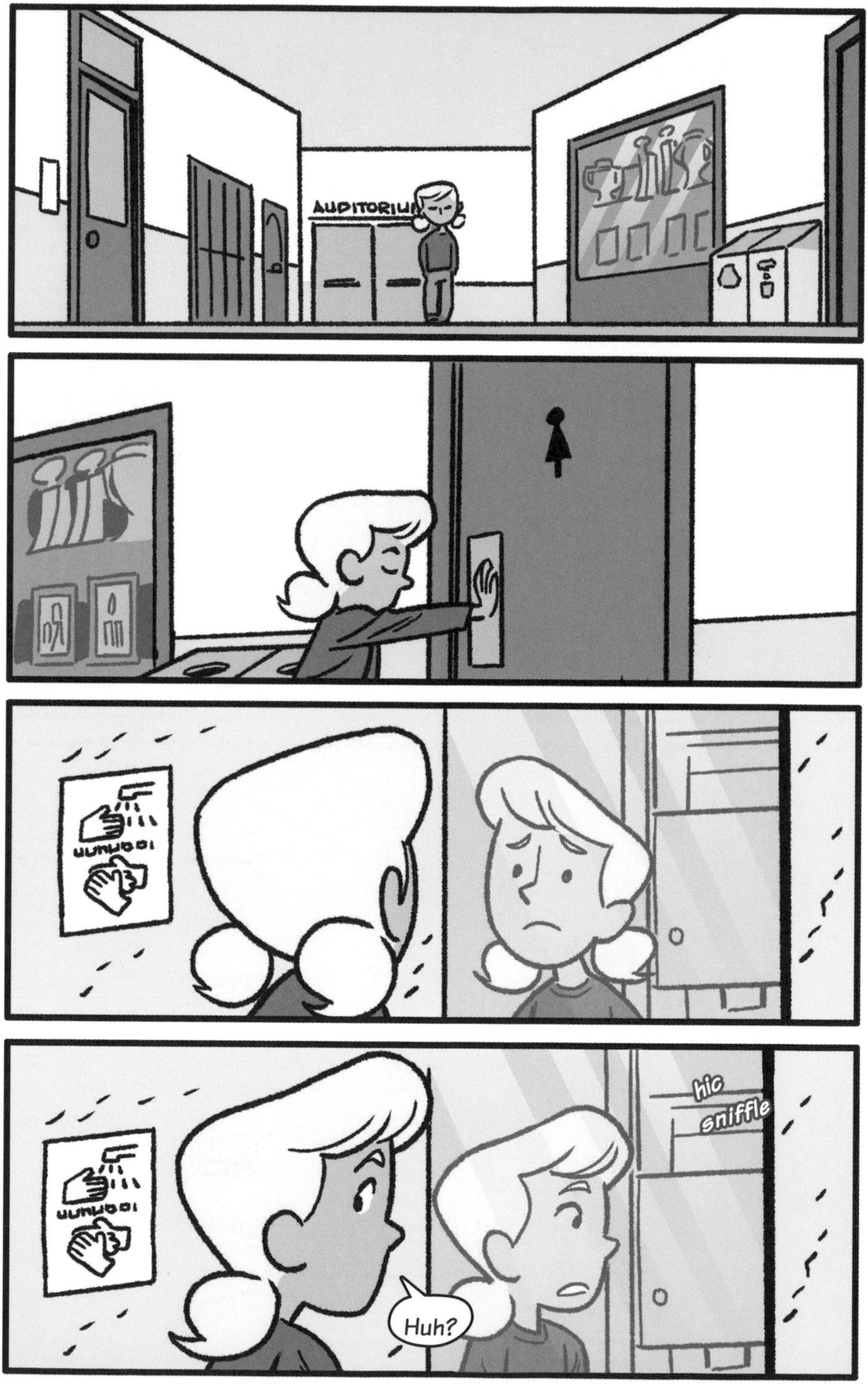
AUDITORIU
hic
sniffle
Huh?

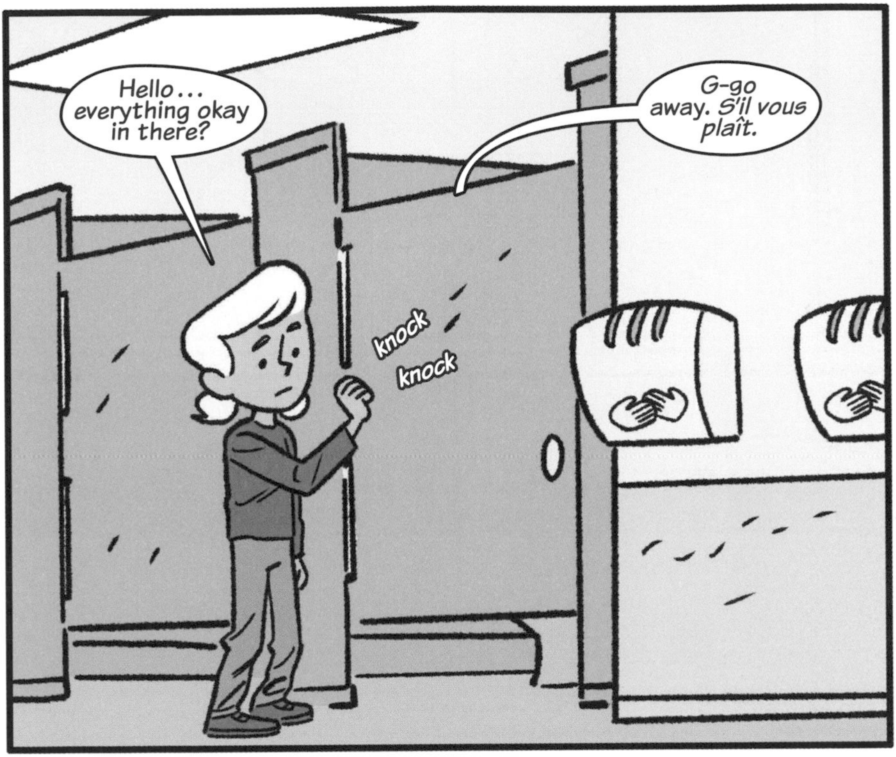
Hello... everything okay in there?
G-go away. S'il vous plaît.
knock
knock

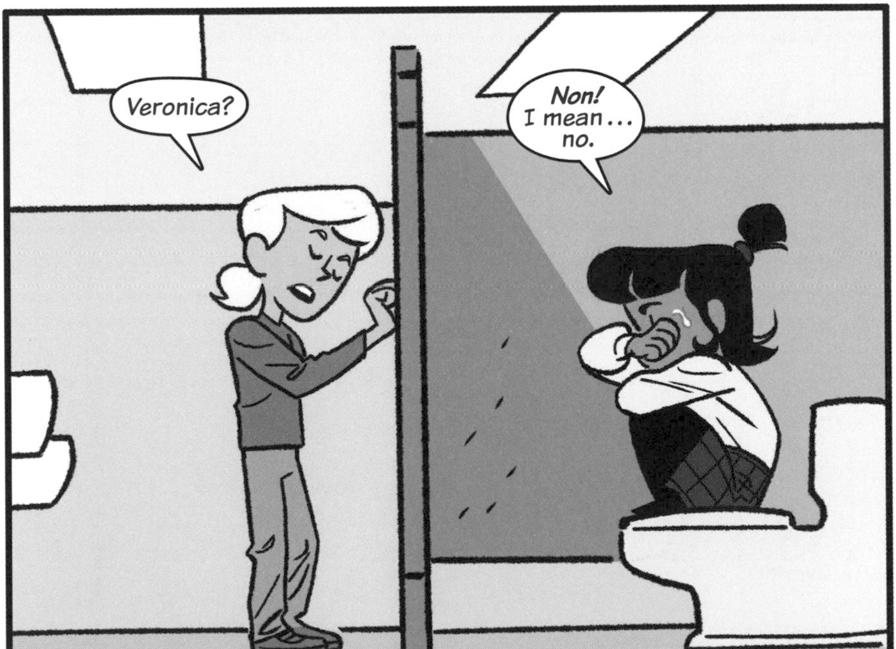
Veronica?
Non! I mean... no.

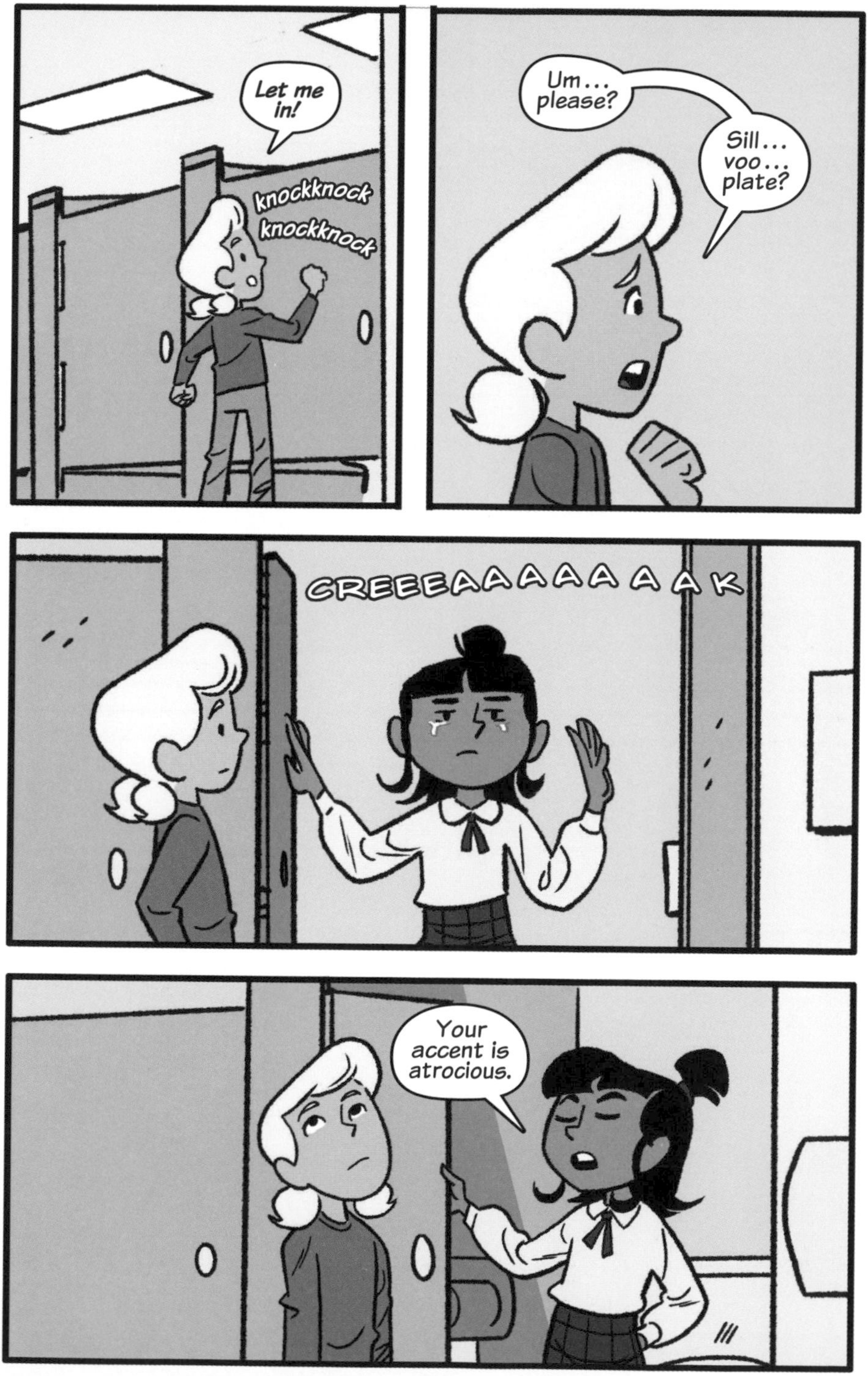
Let me in!
knockknock
knockknock
Um... please?
Sill... voo... plate?
CREEEAAAAAAAK
Your accent is atrocious.

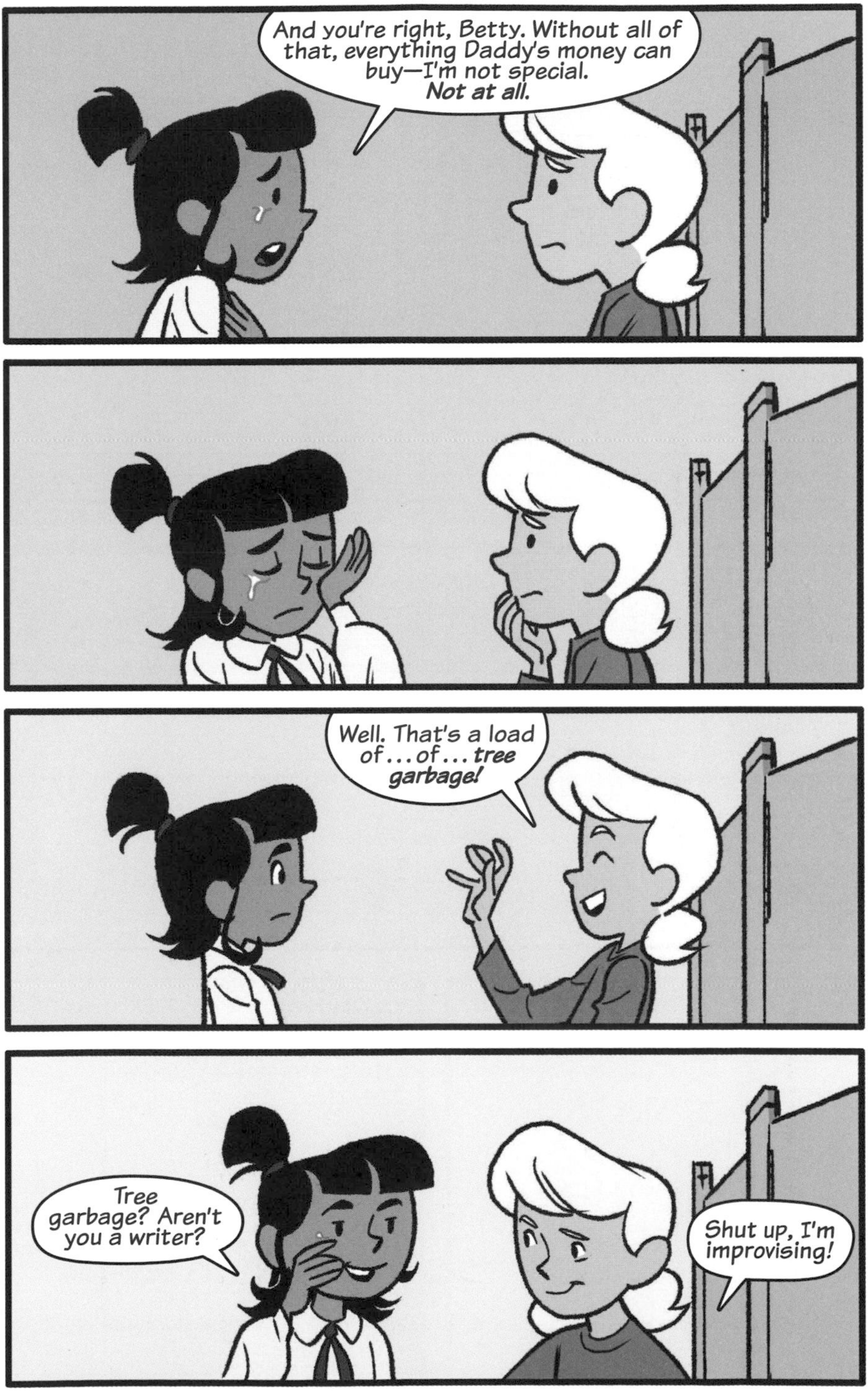
And you're right, Betty. Without all of that, everything Daddy's money can buy—I'm not special. **Not at all.**
Well. That's a load of . . . of . . . ***tree garbage!***
Tree garbage? Aren't you a writer?
Shut up, I'm improvising!

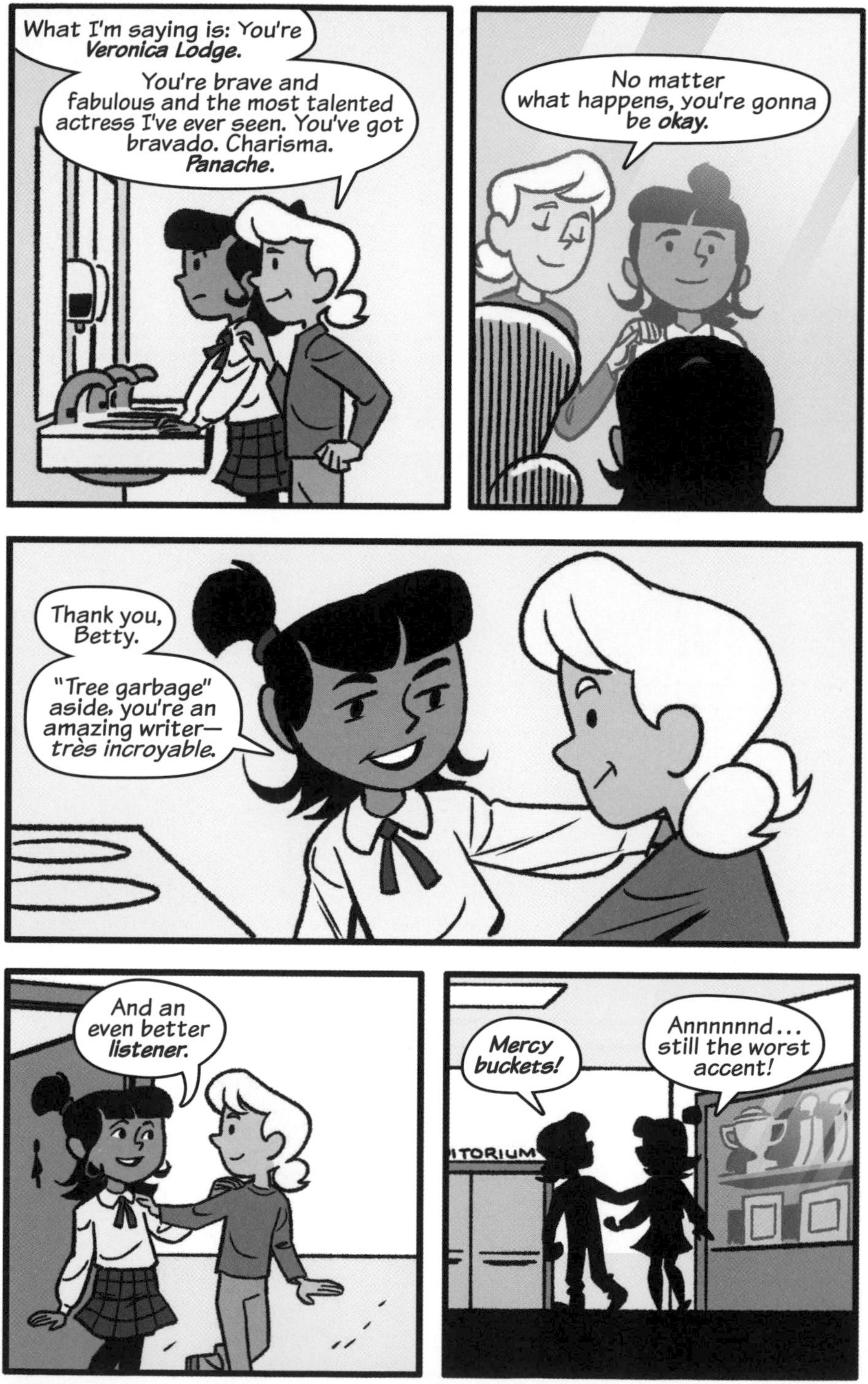
What I'm saying is: You're *Veronica Lodge.*
You're brave and fabulous and the most talented actress I've ever seen. You've got bravado. Charisma. *Panache.*
No matter what happens, you're gonna be *okay.*
Thank you, Betty.
"Tree garbage" aside, you're an amazing writer— *très incroyable.*
And an even better *listener.*
ITORIUM
Mercy buckets!
Annnnnnd... still the worst accent!

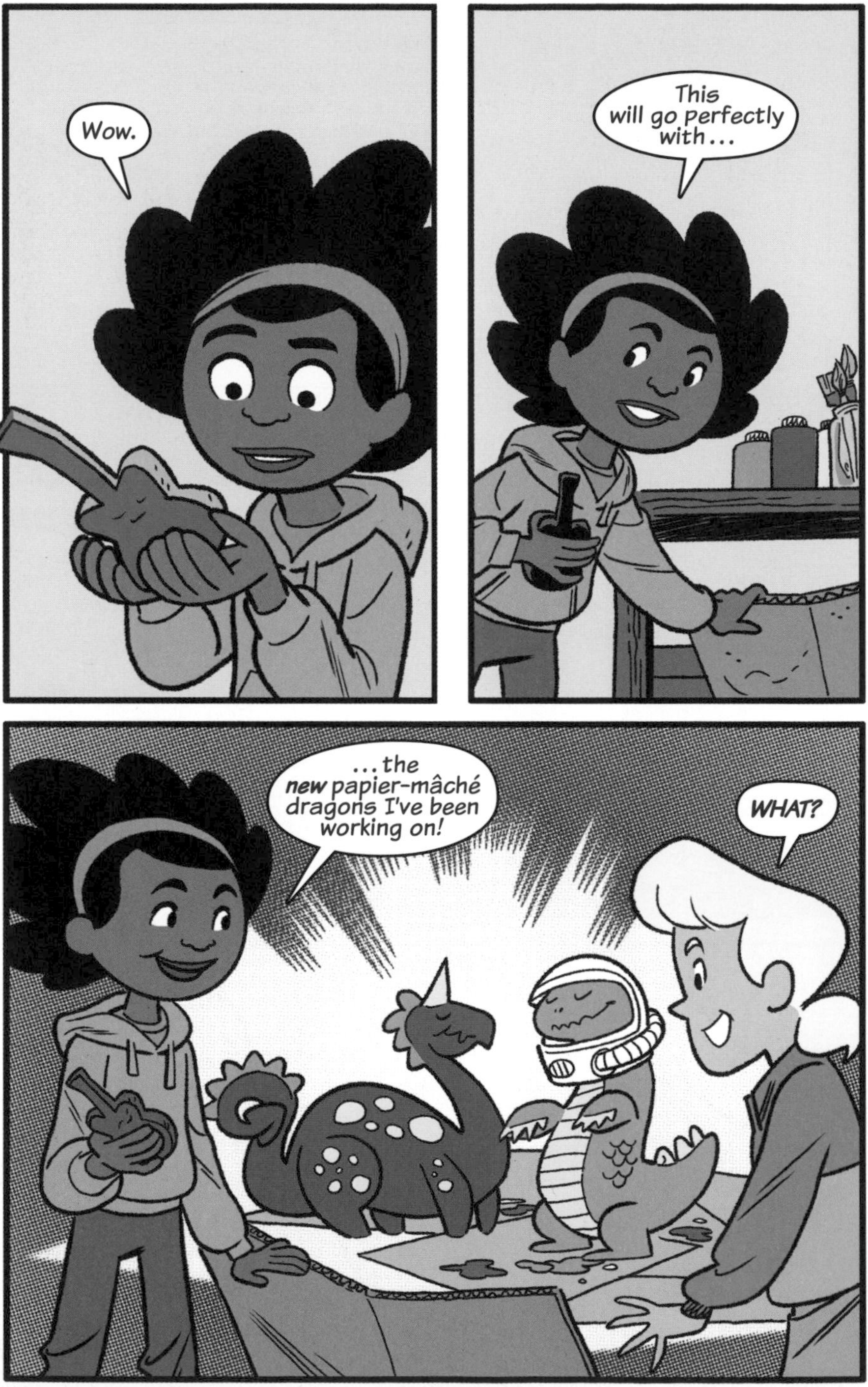
Wow.
This will go perfectly with...
...the *new* papier-mâché dragons I've been working on!
WHAT?

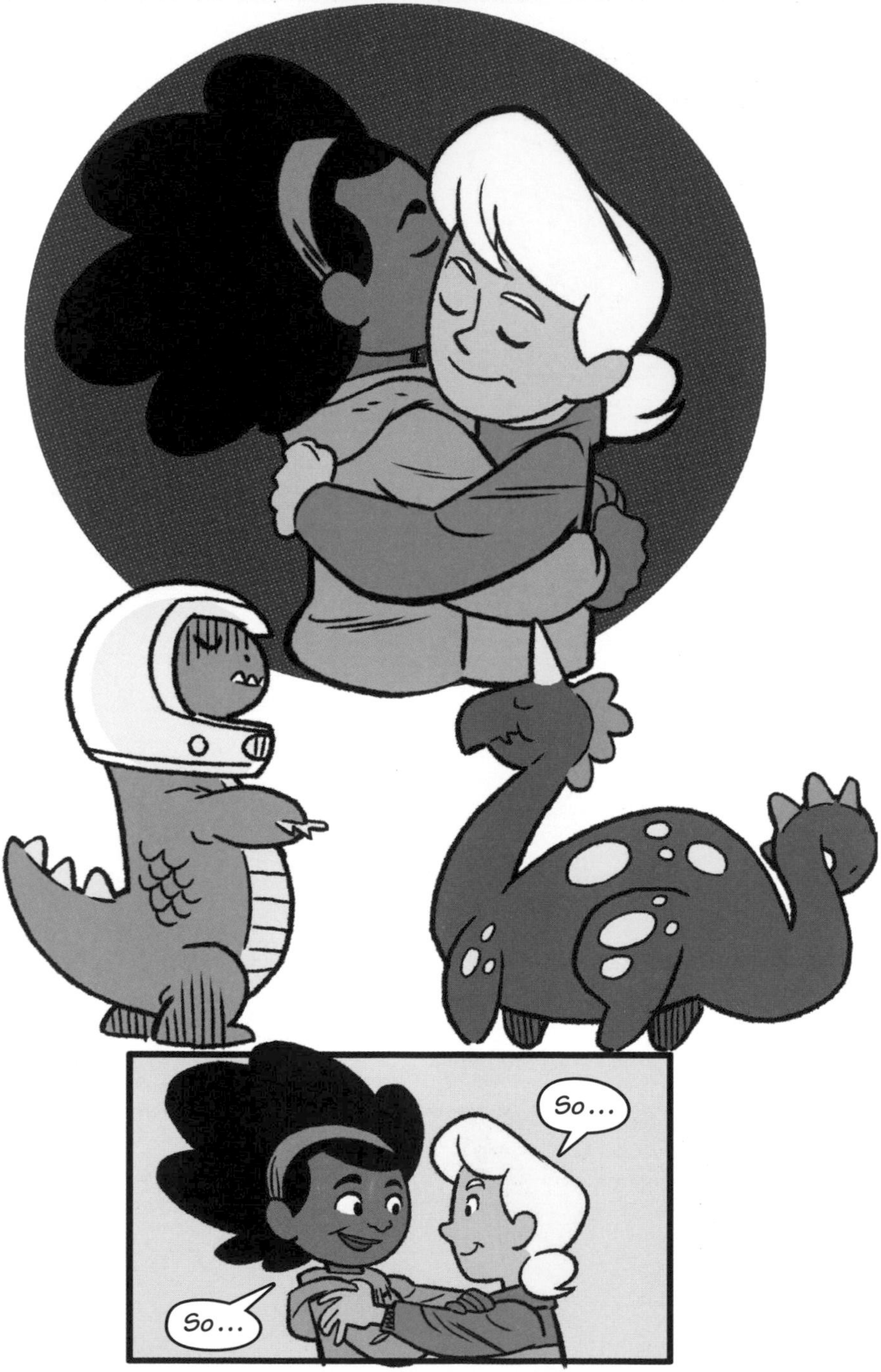
So...
So...

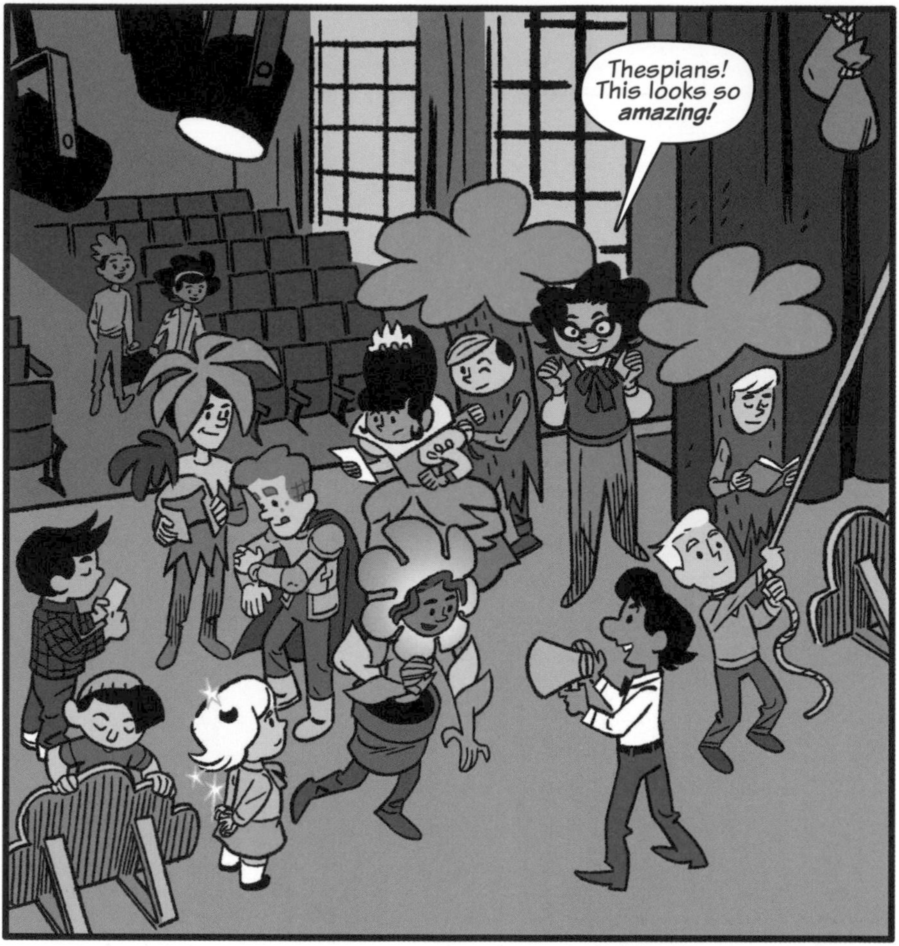
Thespians! This looks so *amazing!*

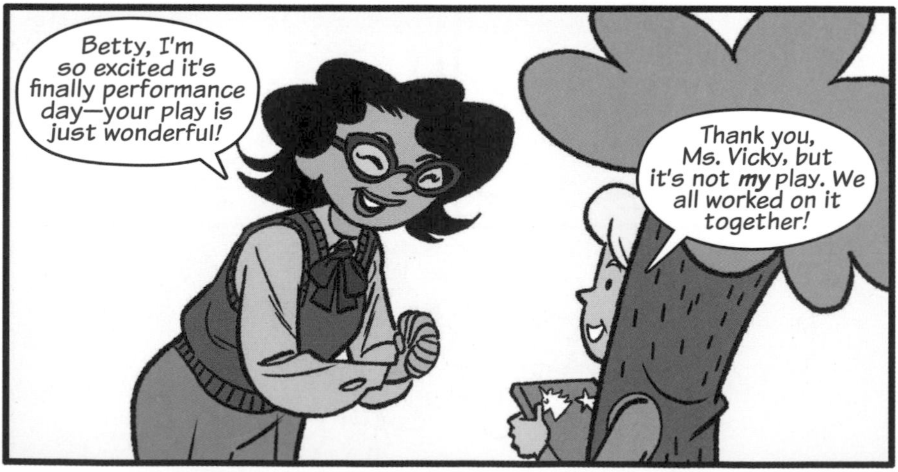
Betty, I'm so excited it's finally performance day—your play is just wonderful!
Thank you, Ms. Vicky, but it's not *my* play. We all worked on it together!

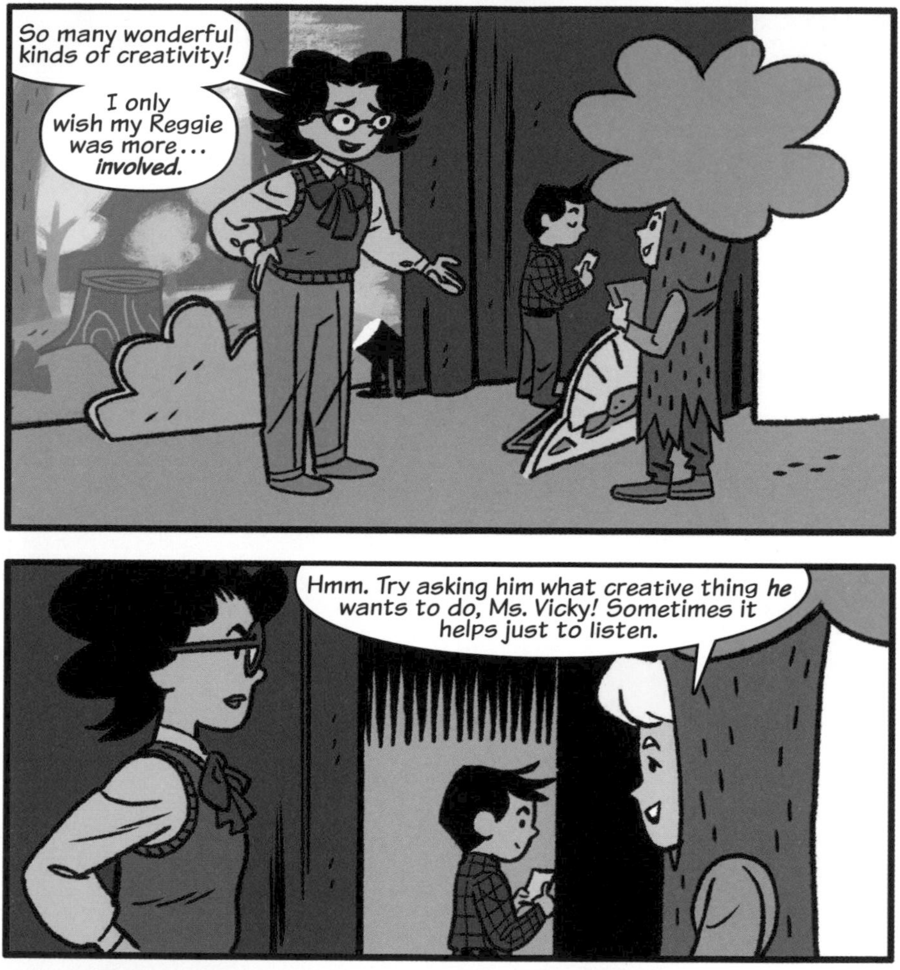

So many wonderful kinds of creativity!
I only wish my Reggie was more… *involved.*
Hmm. Try asking him what creative thing *he* wants to do, Ms. Vicky! Sometimes it helps just to listen.
Hey…
Hey…

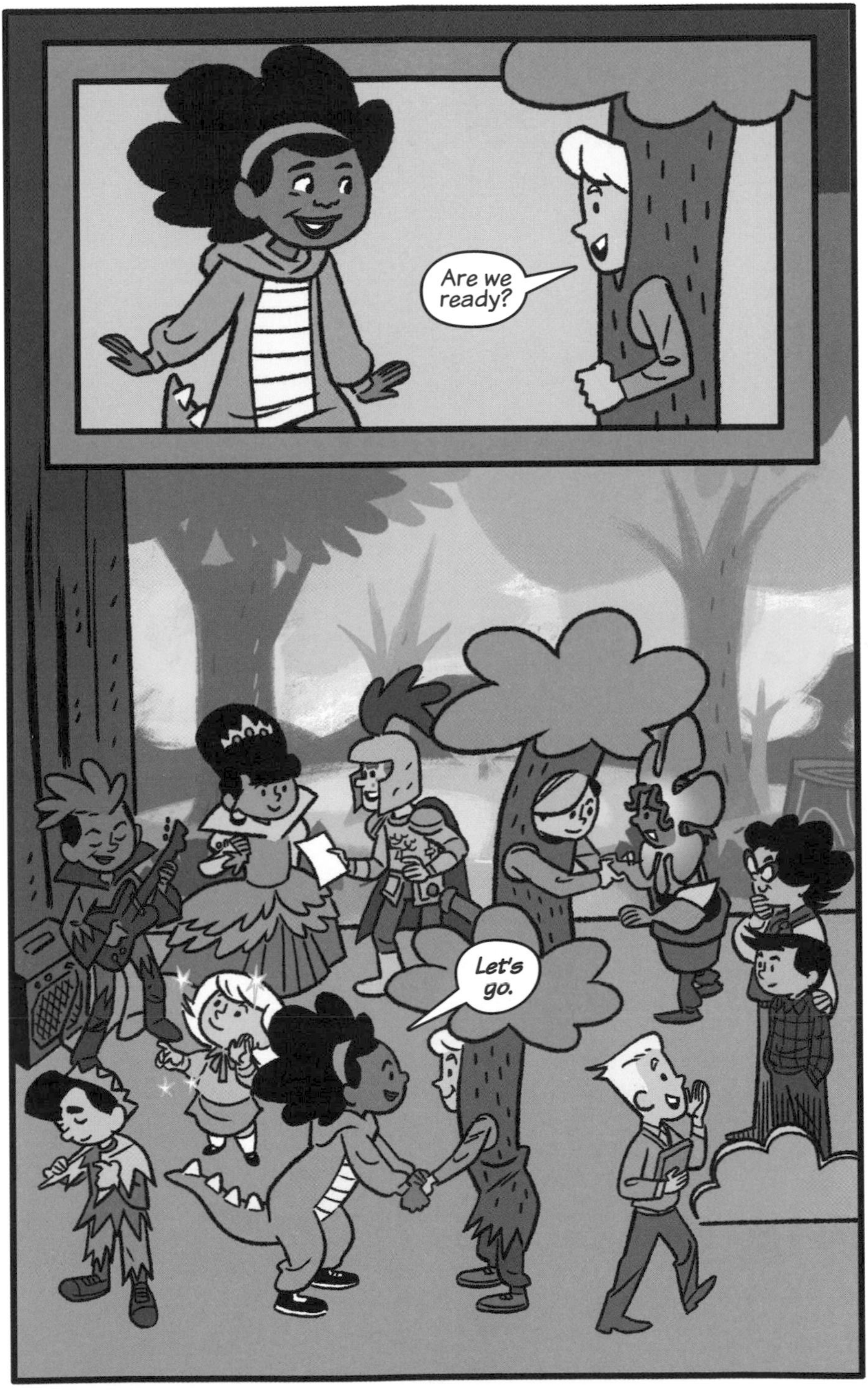
Are we ready?
Let's go.

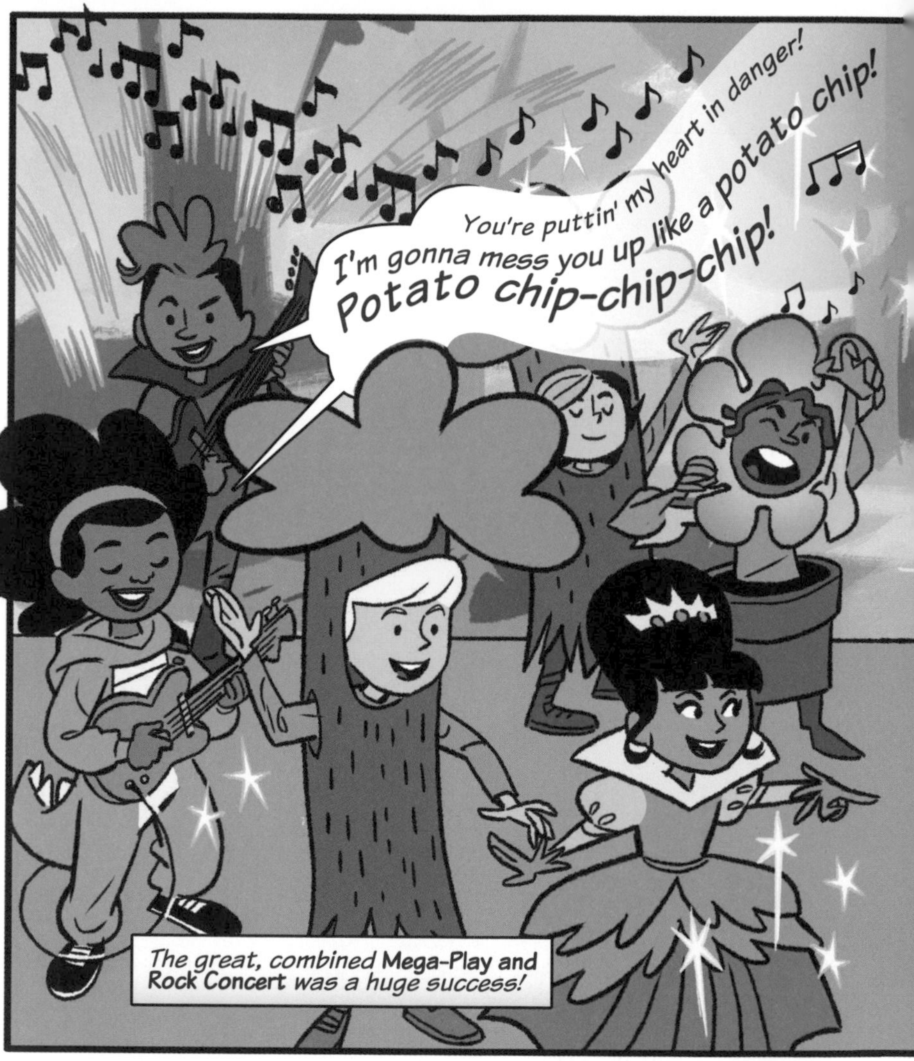
You're puttin' my heart in danger!
I'm gonna mess you up like a potato chip!
Potato chip-chip-chip!
The great, combined Mega-Play and Rock Concert was a huge success!

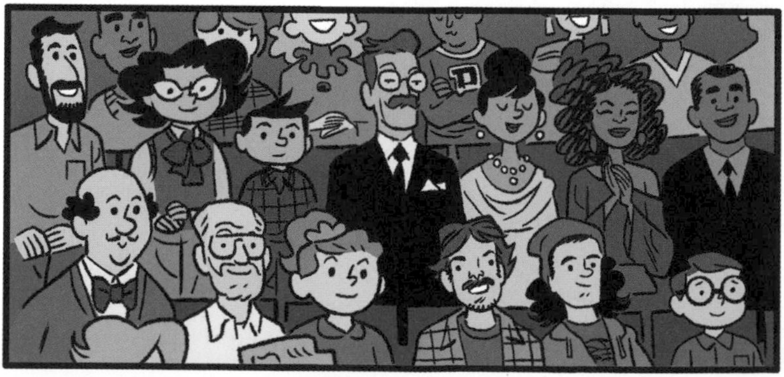

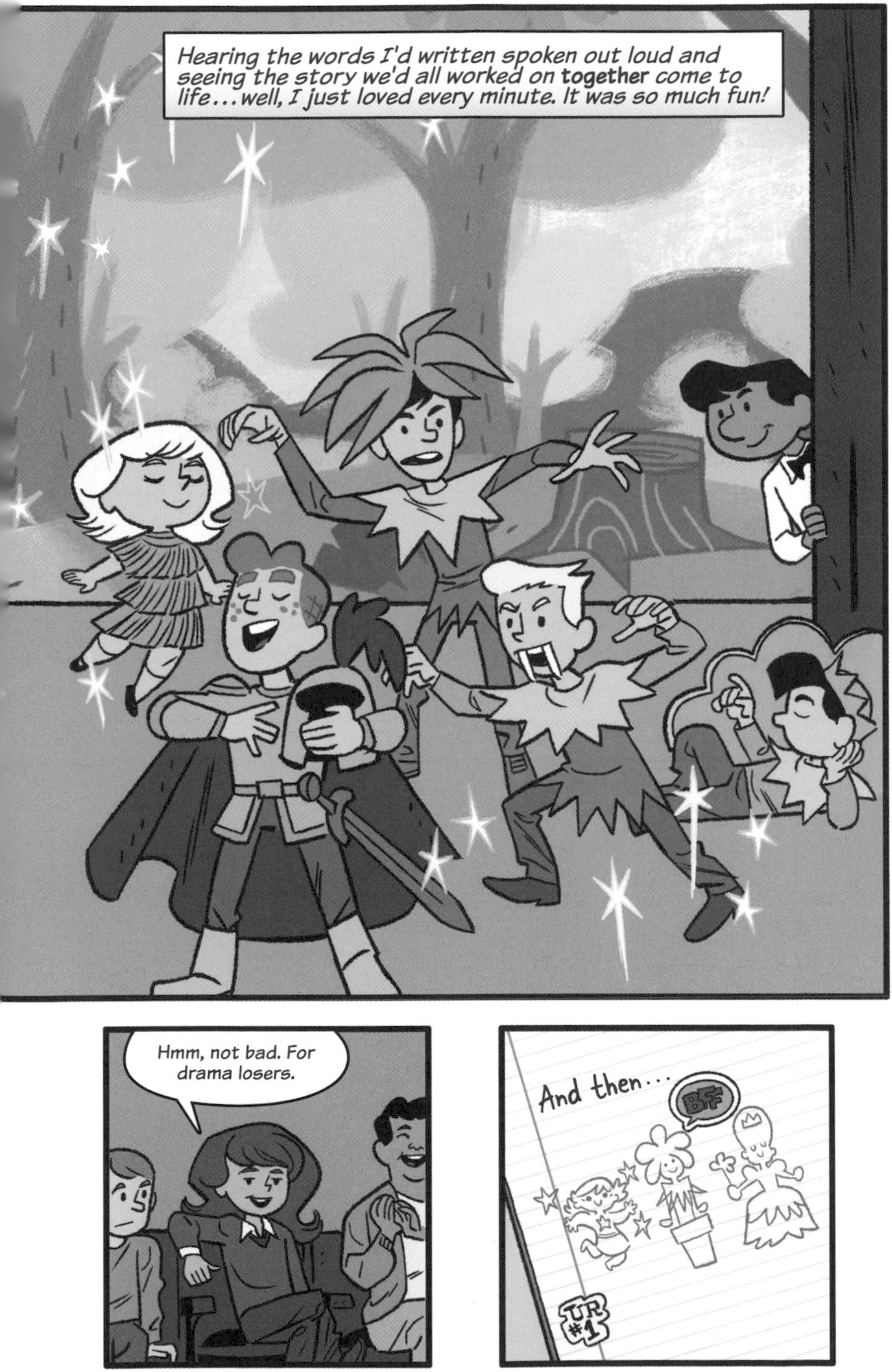
Hearing the words I'd written spoken out loud and seeing the story we'd all worked on **together** come to life... well, I just loved every minute. It was so much fun!
Hmm, not bad. For drama losers.
And then...
BFF
UR #1

ACKNOWLEDGMENTS

As a lifelong fan of Betty, Valerie, Veronica, and the whole Archie Comics gang, it was a thrill to get to write these kids. Thank you to my awesome collaborator, J. Bone, and to our fabulous editor, Rachel Gluckstern, for playing with me in this world and bringing it to life so beautifully. Thank you to my agent, Diana Fox, for working your usual magic, and to Bethany Bryan for knowing that we girls can do anything. Thank you to everyone at Little Bee Books and Archie Comics for all the work and love you put into this book. My communities make me who I am, so thank you to all the denizens of my personal Sparklespacelandia: the Girl Gang(s), the Shamers, TRB crew, Heroine Club, the Kuhn-Yoneyama-Chen-Coffeys, and the incredible Asian American arts community of LA. And a special shout-out to Team Batgirl, Sara Miller and Nicole Goux: You made me a better comics writer, and I can't thank you enough. And thank you to Jeff Chen, my most favorite Dragon Scientist Knight of all. I love you. —*Sarah Kuhn*

First of all, I want to thank Rachel Gluckstern for inviting me into this project, and to Sarah Kuhn for writing a fun story with so much drahhh-maaahh. My thanks to Jaime Gelman and Rob Wall for catching my early mistakes and making sure the book looks so good. Penciling and inking 122 pages was a massive undertaking and I would have gone crazy by the time I got to the colors if not for the help of Riely McFarlane, who flatted a gajillion layers for me. Thank you to Danny B., who helped keep me going with weekly tea and comic breaks. Thank you also to Cliff for regular video chats that had nothing to do with comic books. I shared many stressed-out deadline chats with my equally under pressure writer friend Rachelle. I'm grateful for our friendship and shared love of WS. I want to thank Dan Parent, who pulled me into the working world of Archie Comics when we teamed up to draw Kevin Keller however many years ago. And my thanks to Darwyn Cooke, who I talk to every day even though he's not here to listen anymore. —*J. Bone*

ABOUT THE WRITER

Sarah Kuhn is the writer of the critically acclaimed teen graphic novel *Shadow of the Batgirl* for DC Comics. Her teen novel debut, the Japan-set romantic comedy *I Love You So Mochi*, was a Junior Library Guild selection and a nominee for YALSA's Best Fiction for Young Adults. She has also penned a variety of short fiction and comics, including a series of Barbie comics. A third-generation Japanese American, she lives in Los Angeles with her husband and a closet overflowing with vintage treasures.

ABOUT THE ARTIST

J. Bone is an Eisner-nominated comics veteran. He's perhaps best known for his work on *The Spirit* and *The New Frontier*, both from DC Comics, and *Spider-Man's Tangled Web* from Marvel Comics. Most recently, J. Bone has been inking a number of Archie projects, including a Kevin Keller miniseries and *Archie Meets Batman '66*.